December *to* Remember

BOB LEONE

ISBN 979-8-89345-541-0 (paperback)
ISBN 979-8-89345-542-7 (digital)

Christian Faith Publishing
832 Park Avenue
Meadville, PA 16335
www.christianfaithpublishing.com

Printed in the United States of America

To Angelo Panetta, mentor and friend

Foreword

A heart-tugging family drama, *December to Remember* is a story that will make you laugh, make you cry, and encourage and enhance your prayer life all at the same time. One of the things I love about author Bob Leone is that all his stories contain an element of prayer, and this one is no different. Leone's faith shows us that through God, anything is possible, especially when you ask, simply through the act of prayer.

Bob Leone uses the character of Grace, the matriarch in the story, to show us that God is gracious, our comforter, and His answers are always yes, no, or not right now. Through the hardships in the Gerard family, we see God's glory through grace, His hand in little Ella's artwork, His heart in the way Hannah writes music, and His love between a father and his children with John and Abigail. This is a story about faith, prayer, and a close-knit family dynamic. *December to Remember* encourages the reader while showcasing how a family perseveres through adversity with the hope and love of Jesus.

Once you finish reading *December to Remember*, this beautiful, prayer-filled family drama will leave you wanting to know more about Him.

Melissa Goad
Award-winning director, actor, and producer known for *They Don't Cast Shadows* (2021)

Other Books by the Author

The Shadow series:

- *They Don't Cast Shadows: Book 1* (now a feature film)
- *More Than Just Shadows: Book 2*
- *Terror in the Shadows: Book 3*

The Heart series:

- Novella—*His Unfaithful Heart* (in preproduction for a feature film)
- Novella—*An Obsessive Heart*
- Novella—*The Right Heart*
- Novella—*Her Christmas Heart*
- Novella—*His Fiery Heart*

Heart Series collection:

- *Gathering of Hearts* (includes a collection of all five novellas)

Cast of Characters

John Gerard—the Gerard family father
Grace Gerard—John's wife
Abby Gerard–Anderson—John and Grace's oldest daughter
James Anderson—Abby's husband
Hannah Gerard—John and Grace's middle daughter
Derek—Hannah's ex-boyfriend
Travis—Hannah's fiancé
Ella—John and Grace's youngest daughter

Chapter 1

In the warmly lit office of Pastor Elijah Wilson, Grace and John Gerard sat facing him, their expressions a mix of worry and courage. The room, with its neatly lined bookshelves and the gentle sunlight streaming in, seemed almost too peaceful for the gravity of their conversation.

Grace Gerard, at forty-eight, embodied a cheerful spirit in her petite frame. Her smile was a beacon of light in any space she graced. Her life was a beautiful tapestry woven with threads of love, family, and resilience that stood unshaken. Grace's heart beats for her dear husband, John, and their three treasured daughters to whom she dedicated her endless love and care.

Her spiritual journey had begun in a quaint Sunday School when she was just seven. Amidst the innocent laughter of children and captivating Bible tales, Grace found Jesus. This pivotal moment was deeply engraved in her soul, marking the start of an unwavering commitment to her faith.

At the tender age of twelve, Grace's world was shadowed by a somber reality: the mortality of her parents. This memory was a heavy cloak upon her young shoulders, profoundly shaping her life's path. Growing up, she was acutely aware of the fleeting nature of life, witnessing her parents' gradual decline. First, her father, Martin, succumbed to lung cancer, followed closely by her mother, Simone, who passed from the same illness. Both were avid lovers of the great outdoors, their passion for camping and water sports only matched by their unfortunate indulgence in cigarette smoking. Grace's childhood home had always been shrouded in the haze of tobacco smoke.

Despite never touching a cigarette herself, fate dealt Grace a cruel hand. She was diagnosed with the same ailment that claimed her parents: lung cancer.

But today, in the stillness of the pastor's office, with her voice barely above a whisper and her eyes shimmering with restrained weeping, Grace said, "Pastor, it's just…it all feels unreal. Too fast." John nodded slowly, gently holding her hand.

Pastor Wilson, his silver hair a testament to a lifetime of guidance and compassion, leaned forward, his voice a calming balm in the storm of emotions. "I understand," he said gently, his eyes reflecting a deep well of empathy. "Such news can indeed be daunting, like a tsunami hitting without warning."

John, gripping Grace's hand a little tighter, looked at the pastor with a searching gaze. "But how do we deal with this? It feels like we're in uncharted waters."

"With faith, John, and the strength you draw from each other," the pastor replied gently. "You're not alone in this."

Grace wiped a tear that escaped her eye, her voice trembling. "I'm so scared, but not for myself. I know where I'm going, but for John, for our girls…"

"It's natural to feel scared. But remember, in times of fear, your faith is a lighthouse in the storm," Pastor Wilson said with a comforting tone.

John leaned forward, his voice a mix of despair and hope. "Do you believe there's a reason for all this, Pastor? A purpose we can't see?"

Pastor Wilson nodded thoughtfully. "Life's trials often seem senseless, John. But the Bible teaches us that there's a bigger plan, even when it's hidden from our view."

Grace's face softened slightly, a faint glimmer of hope appearing in her eyes. "I want to hold onto hope to make the most of the time we have."

"That's a powerful way to see it. Cherish each moment and find joy in the small things. That's how you navigate through this," Pastor Wilson advised with a warm smile on his face.

John squeezed Grace's hand, their fingers intertwining. "We'll face this together, no matter what."

"And you're not alone," Pastor Wilson reassured. "The Lord is with you, and the love you share, the support of your family, it's your anchor."

Grace and John exchanged a look, their determination growing. John spoke firmly, "We'll tell the girls at Christmas. Have them all home."

Grace whispered, head bowed, "I want to spend our Christmas together." Grace patted her tear-filled eyes. "In joy and happiness, not under the shroud of sorrow."

Pastor Wilson offered a gentle, reassuring smile. "Keep the faith. Let's pray for strength and understanding of the Lord's will in all of this."

*****

In the heart of New York City, under the glow of eternal city lights, Abigail "Abby" Gerard-Anderson and her husband, James Anderson, found solace in their modest apartment. As the night embraced the city, their home became a sanctuary amidst the urban chaos. Abby leaned into James, her head resting gently against his shoulder.

"Remember the stars in the night sky in Nashville?" Abby whispered, her voice tinged with nostalgia. She had left behind her charming hometown, where she grew up as the eldest of three Gerard sisters, a born leader with a fiery ambition. "Here you can barely see the moon."

James looked down at her, his eyes softening. "You've always been destined for great things. Your family must be so proud," he said, recalling her graduation from college with a degree in graphic design.

Abby chuckled softly. "My family back home are proud of me. But this," she gestured around the cozy room and held her now bulging belly, "this is my greatest adventure. New York, you, the baby, everything."

James, raised in a world of privilege, contrasted starkly with Abby's self-made path. Yet it was his grounded nature and passion for justice that drew Abby to him. As a defense lawyer, he fought for the underprivileged, a trait that made him even more endearing to her.

Their love story had begun when James's sister, Julie, introduced them. Julie, Abby's roommate and colleague at an interior design magazine, had unwittingly played cupid. James had been captivated by Abby from the moment they met, certain they were meant to be.

Their relationship flourished over time, deepening into a profound connection. James, unable to contain his love, had proposed a year ago, and Abby had joyously agreed. Their wedding plans were a testament to their shared dreams and aspirations.

Meeting James's family had been a seamless transition. They had accepted Abby instantly, recognizing in her the same values of justice, compassion, and advocacy for the underdog that they cherished.

Now in their little world, Abby and James found peace away from the city's relentless pulse. Lost watching a movie on their television, the room around them was alive with flickering shadows, a cocoon of intimacy in the vast expanse of New York.

Abby sighed contentedly. "I love our life, our little corner in this big, crazy city." James pulled her closer. "As long as I'm with you, every place feels like home."

Outside, the city continued its restless dance, but inside, Abby and James reveled in their own universe, built on love, dreams, and a deep unshakeable bond.

Abby, four months pregnant, rested her head against James's shoulder, feeling the comforting warmth of his body. She smiled softly, her hand resting gently on her slightly rounded belly. The sensation of the little life growing inside her was both exhilarating and daunting.

James looked down at her, his eyes filled with a mixture of awe and love. "Can you believe it? We're going to be parents," he whispered, his voice filled with emotion.

Abby's eyes shimmered with unshed tears as she nodded. "It's like a dream, isn't it? In this huge city, amidst all this chaos, we have our little miracle." Her voice was a soft murmur, filled with wonder.

James gently cupped her face in his hands, bringing his forehead to rest against hers. "You're going to be an amazing mother, Abby. I can't wait to see you holding our baby."

Abby laughed, a sound filled with joy and a hint of nervousness. "And you, an incredible father. I just hope I can be half as good as my mom was."

James's embrace tightened, a protective and reassuring gesture. "You will be. We'll figure it out together. We always do."

In that moment, with the city's heartbeat echoing around them and the glow of the screen illuminating their faces, Abby and James shared a profound connection. They were two souls, bound together in love and anticipation, ready to embark on the greatest adventure of their lives.

The unexpected trill of Abby's phone sliced through their tranquility. Her eyes flickered to the caller ID, a familiar and comforting name. "It's my mom," she murmured, her voice a blend of curiosity and warmth.

With a gesture inviting James into the conversation, Abby activated the speakerphone and greeted her mother. "Hey, Mom."

A pause, a breath. Her mother's voice, usually so sure, now held a note of hesitance. "Abby, dear," she began, "I have a request. Could you and James join us for Christmas this year?"

The question hung in the air, unexpected and intriguing. Abby and James shared a glance, a silent conversation in their eyes. Their tradition was to alternate holidays between families, and this year it was meant to be with James's parents. "Is something the matter, Mom? Why this sudden change?" Abby inquired, her brow furrowed in concern.

Her mother's voice wavered, revealing an undercurrent of urgency. "It's difficult to explain over the phone. But it's important, Abby. Very important. Your father and I would be so grateful if you and James could be here."

Abby's heart quickened with a mix of curiosity and concern. She felt James's frustration, his desires clashing with this unexpected request. The call ended, leaving them in a sea of unspoken thoughts.

James exhaled, a sound heavy with disappointment. "You know how much I've been looking forward to spending Christmas with my family. And with work… Harrison's pressure over the Inglewood case could be a turning point in my career."

Abby's hand found his, a gesture of understanding and support. "I know. But there is something compelling in my mom's voice. Can we find a way to figure this out together?"

He was torn, caught between familial expectations and professional obligations. "I hate to miss this chance with my parents, but the case…it could lead to a senior partnership."

"It's not just about the firm. It's about us, our future," Abby replied, her voice gentle yet firm.

James's gaze met hers, filled with sorrow. "You should go to your mom. It sounds important. We'll have our own celebration when you're back."

Their kiss was a soft promise, a bond that wouldn't be broken by distance. As Abby placed his hand on her stomach, a symbol of their growing family, James's smile was tender, filled with hope and love.

"We'll have plenty of Christmases together, as a family," Abby whispered, her eyes twinkling with tears of joy.

James looked at her, his eyes reflecting the dreams of their future. "As a new family."

As they returned to their movie, the decision hung between them, a poignant reminder of the sacrifices and choices life sometimes demands, even amidst the magic of the holiday season.

*****

In the warm embrace of a close-knit Tennessee family, Hannah Gerard, at twenty-three, blossomed as a middle child of John and Grace Gerard. Her role in the family was more than just filling a space; she was the heart, always there to smooth over any rough patches with her innate empathy and warmth.

Hannah's life was a melody, written early on with the strum of a guitar. Recognizing her natural flair for music, her parents gifted her a guitar, which became the vessel for her growing passion. Each chord she played was a step deeper into a world of musical artistry and soulful expression.

Celebrating a major achievement, Hannah proudly walked onto the stage to receive her Bachelor of Music degree six months ago. This moment was the fruit of her relentless dedication and love for her craft, marking a significant milestone in her life.

College for Hannah wasn't just about academics; it was also where she and Derek Taylor, a childhood friend turned boyfriend, wove a tapestry of love and shared aspirations. Derek, an aspiring actor with a deep appreciation for music, dreamed of a future where they could blend their artistic passions.

Together, they painted a canvas filled with the bright colors of love and artistic dreams.

But the melody of life can be unpredictable, as Hannah discovered on graduation day. Derek, caught in the crosswinds of his acting ambitions and his love for her, chose his career, leaving Hannah heartbroken. The future they had envisioned together shattered in an instant.

Yet Hannah didn't retreat to the familiarity of her Tennessee roots. Instead she sought refuge in the vast, untouched beauty of Montana. Where her cousin, Francine Lindstrom, had a small cattle ranch. There, Hannah believed, in the open arms of nature, she could heal and complete a song that had been growing in her heart. Montana became her haven, a place to rediscover herself amid its majestic landscapes.

In Montana, Hannah's guitar was her anchor, soothing her with its strings and fortifying her with its melodies. Each strum was an outpouring of her emotions, resulting in songs that resonated with audiences in small bars and during karaoke nights at small venues. These performances were not just gigs; they had been declarations of her resilience and determination.

Now on the ranch's porch steps in Montana, under the glow of the setting sun, Hannah abruptly stopped playing her guitar.

"Why did you stop playing?" Francine asked. "Your singing is so beautiful."

"I didn't notice this before, but no frogs," Hannah said, her head tilted to one side.

"What are you talking about? In the first place it's winter, they're hibernating. And secondly, we're miles away from any creek or pond."

"I know that. It's just—"

"Missing home? Derek?"

Hannah didn't reply; she just played her guitar. Each note was a reflection of the tumult in her heart, a quiet anthem to her journey of heartbreak and healing.

Francine sat beside her, her eyes kind and knowing. "You're really putting your soul into that guitar, huh, Hannah?"

Hannah glanced up, her eyes glistening. "It's like the music knows, Fran. It knows what I can't say."

Francine leaned back, watching the star-filled sky. "Music is like that. It speaks when words fail us."

Hannah hesitated, her fingers caressing the guitar strings. "Everything's different now. Derek and I… We had something special. Losing that feels like losing a part of myself."

Francine's expression was tender, her voice a gentle murmur. "Loss can reshape us. It's painful, yet it's also the soil for new beginnings." She glanced at Hannah's engagement ring. "You're starting a new chapter now, embracing new possibilities."

Under the emerging stars, Hannah strummed softly. "I care for Travis, yet thoughts of Derek linger. Does that make me fickle?"

With a reassuring touch on Hannah's shoulder, Francine smiled. "No, it makes you human. Tonight, let the music and stars soothe you. They hold secrets and answers, if you're willing to listen."

Suddenly, Hannah's phone buzzed. She frowned at the caller ID. "It's Mom. Why would she be calling this late?"

Francine's presence was comforting. "There's only one way to find out."

Hannah answered, concern edging her voice. "Mom? Is everything okay?"

"Dear, you need to come home for Christmas. It's urgent." Her mother's voice was tense. Hannah exchanged a worried look with Francine. "But, Mom, I…"

"Your father and I need you, Hannah. Please." With a heavy heart, Hannah agreed. "I'll be there."

Hannah disconnected the call. "That was my mother. She wants me to come home."

"You look worried. Is everything okay?"

"I don't know. Mom said it was important that I come home."

Francine offered a reassuring smile. "Family's always there, no matter the tune life plays."

Hannah sighed, her gaze drifting to the new engagement ring on her finger. "I've got to tell Travis about this change."

As Francine left her to privacy, Hannah reflected on meeting Travis. Hannah had been able to compose a few songs during her time in Montana and even played a few gigs in the local bars and open-mic karaoke venues in the city of Billings. It was in one of these bars she met Travis Becker, a handsome cowboy who swept her off her feet during a low time in her life. A month ago, Travis had proposed, and she accepted.

Dialing Travis, she braced herself. "Hey, I can't make it for Christmas."

Travis's voice, tinged with a distinct cowboy drawl, carried a note of confusion. "What's goin' on? Everythin' all right?"

"It's my family. They need me to come home."

A hint of frustration colored his tone. "But shoot, my folks are countin' on us bein' there."

"I'm sorry, Travis. I have to go to Nashville."

You could almost hear the irritation in Travis's voice, thick as molasses. "Darn it, I don't rightly know what I'm gonna tell my folks."

"Sorry." Hannah hung up, feeling torn. She returned to her guitar, her emotions spilling into her music, blending with the Montana landscape's serene beauty.

Chapter 2

Hannah and Abby purposely scheduled their flights to arrive at Nashville International Airport at nearly the same time. Upon their arrival, they planned to meet near the baggage claim. As Hannah came into the terminal from the airplane ramp, she rolled her suitcase behind her, her guitar bag strapped to her back gently bumping her as she walked. She saw her sister, and she quickened her steps. Both grinning from ear to ear, they gave each other a warm sisterly hug after months of not physically seeing each other.

Hannah glanced down at Abby's stomach. "Ah, you're beginning to show."

"Almost four months along." She turned to the side. "Not too noticeable, is it?"

Hannah laughed. "Not really. You should be proud, not ashamed of it. You're married, after all." Abby smiled.

"Not ashamed, just a little self-conscience, that's all."

Abby glanced down at Hannah's ring. "Well, it won't be long until you're married."

Hannah sighed. "True."

Abby and Hannah walked to the outside curb. A white compact car with an Uber sign on it pulled up.

"Here's our ride," Abby said.

*****

The December air was crisp and cool as the Uber car made its way down the Nashville highway, its wheels humming a steady rhythm on the asphalt. Inside, Hannah gazed out of the window, the twinkling lights of the city reflecting in her light brown eyes and her mind wandering through the maze of memories this city held. Beside her, Abby gazed out the opposite window, lost in her thoughts.

Hannah's thoughts drifted back to their childhood home nestled on the outskirts of Nashville. She remembered the sprawling backyard, the treehouse where countless secrets were shared, and the laughter that always seemed to fill their home. Their childhood was something out of a storybook, filled with adventure and the warmth of family love.

But as the car rolled down the off-ramp, weaving through the streets adorned with festive lights and decorations, a shadow fell over Hannah's heart. Derek. His name alone was enough to stir a whirlpool of emotions within her. Six months had passed since their breakup, yet his memory lingered like a persistent fog, clouding her happiness.

Abby, sensing her sister's shift in mood, turned to her. "Hey, you okay?" she asked, her voice laced with concern.

Hannah forced a smile. "Yeah, just…thinking about old times," she replied, her voice barely above a whisper.

Abby said, "I need a cup of coffee."

Hannah flashed a look of concern. "Is that okay when you're pregnant?"

Abby laughed. "A cup or two is okay." Abby held up her hand as a pledge. "I promise I won't order an expresso."

Hannah glanced out the window. "Up ahead is Sophie's coffee shop."

Abby said to the driver, "Could you pull over so we can grab a cup of coffee?"

"Sure, miss," he replied. "But I can't wait longer than three minutes."

Abby sighed. "It's going to take a little longer than that."

"Sorry, those are the rules I have to go by."

Abby and Hannah gave each other a quick look and, without speaking to each other, directed the driver to take them to the coffee shop.

*****

The driver stopped and opened the trunk of the car and pulled out their rolling suitcases. Abby paid the driver.

As Abby and Hannah walked away with their suitcases in tow, the driver shouted, "Call me if you need a lift."

The two sisters entered the cozy mom-and-pop coffee shop. The scent of fresh coffee filled their senses, and the buzzing of the low hum of conversation and the clinking of cups was music to their ears. They found a spot in a quiet corner, placing their luggage next to the table. As Hannah sat down, visibly tired from the trip, Abby ordered two cups of coffee. She knew her sister's preference without her having to say anything.

Hannah, with a hint of cowboy boots under her jeans and a guitar pick necklace, sat peering out the window. She pulled out her guitar and strummed her guitar softly. Her face carried a mixture of nostalgia and determination.

The door chimed, and Derek Taylor walked in, looking both surprised and hesitant as his gaze landed on Hannah. Their eyes met for the first time since their painful breakup.

Hannah whispered, "Derek…" Hannah's fingers faltered on the guitar strings, the melody dying in the air. Thoughts of their last encounter six months ago race through her mind.

*****

The bench on the campus quad had been bathed in warm sunlight, a stark contrast to the turmoil within Hannah's heart. She sat on a bench, her hands clutching a crumpled letter that Derek had left on her bed. When she had read it, tears ran down her face like the leaky pen Derek had used to scrawl the distressing news. In her other hand, she held the guitar pick necklace, a symbol of her passion for music. Derek, her childhood friend who had been her steady boyfriend for four years, had stood in front of her, his face a mixture of pain and resignation.

Hannah held up the letter that Derek had left her on her bed this morning and, with a shaky voice, asked, "What are you saying, Derek?"

Derek took a deep breath, his eyes avoiding Hannah's. "Hannah, I think we need to break up."

Hannah's world shattered, the words hitting her like a tidal wave. Her voice breaking as she uttered, "What? No, Derek, we're… we're supposed to get married after graduation. We made plans. We talked about our future together."

Derek's gaze remained fixed on the ground, his voice heavy with guilt. He said quietly, "I know we did. But things have changed for me. I need to move on, find my own path."

Hannah's face tightened. "Is there someone else?"

Derek threw up his hands. "No. No, I just feel that we must part and each find our own way. It was fun while it lasted. Can't you just accept that?"

"So I was a distraction from your studies? A plaything to get your jollies?"

Derek said sincerely, "Never. You misunderstand. I do love you."

Hannah's grip on the guitar pick necklace tightened, her heart pounding. Teary-eyed Hannah said, "So what? You're just walking away from everything we had? From us?"

Derek finally met her gaze, his eyes filled with pain. He stood as he struggled to get the words out. "I never wanted to hurt you, Hannah. But I can't ignore this feeling anymore. I need to pursue my career in New York."

Hannah with a trembling voice said, "And what about me? What about what I want?"

Derek's silence spoke volumes, and Hannah's tears fell freely.

In barely a whisper, she said, "You're breaking my heart. After everything we've shared, you're leaving me."

Derek's own eyes glistened with tears not fallen. "I never wanted to hurt you. I think I am doing what is best for both of us."

Hannah's hands had trembled as she clutched the crumpled letter, her dreams unraveling before her.

Sobbing, she had said, "I thought we were building a life together. I thought our dreams aligned."

Derek's expression was a mix of regret and empathy. "I'm so sorry. I never wanted to be the reason for your pain. If I have learned anything from our time together, it is that you are being driven in a different direction than me. You want to write music and perform. I, on the other hand, want to make it on Broadway. Acting is where I am headed."

The weight of the moment hung heavily between them as Hannah's heartbreak had been laid bare.

Derek whispered, "I hope you find happiness, Hannah. You deserve it."

With those words, Derek had turned and walked away, leaving Hannah on the bench; her world had forever changed.

*****

Snapping out of her remembrance of their breakup in college, Hannah set her guitar on the table in the coffee shop as Derek approached her table, his expression a mix of guilt and unease.

Derek said softly, with a little embarrassment, "Hannah."

There was a tense silence as their eyes locked, memories of shared laughter and tears flooding back.

Hannah said, her voice unsure, "I never expected to see you again."

Derek shuffled awkwardly closer. "Yeah, I didn't think I'd ever be back in Nashville."

Hannah's grip on the neck of her guitar tightened as she took a deep breath, summoning her courage. Hannah said, "You left me. After everything we had been through. I thought we were getting married."

Derek shifted uncomfortably, his eyes avoiding hers. He said softly, "I know. And I'm sorry for how it all ended."

Hannah, teary-eyed, said, "You broke my heart, Derek. I left town to find myself, to heal from what you did."

Derek looked remorseful, his own emotions evident. "I regret hurting you, Hannah. But I also needed to figure things out for myself."

Hannah said bitterly, "And did you figure it out? So how was Broadway? Did you make a splash on Broadway? Did you find what you were looking for?"

Derek's silence spoke volumes.

Hannah growled angrily, "I poured my heart and soul into our relationship, into my music, and you walked away like it meant nothing."

Derek said, his voice cracking, "It wasn't that simple. I was lost too."

Hannah's anger softened, replaced by a mix of sadness and resignation. "Broadway wasn't what you expected?"

Derek bowed his head. "Broadway was a bust. I couldn't get any parts. I ran out of money, so now I'm back home. I'm a failure." He paused and took a deep look into her eyes. "I would like to get back together. I see that I was wrong."

Hannah sighed. "I've changed. I've been through a lot these past months. I found my voice again. My music means more to me than ever."

Derek, looking regretfully, said, "I'm glad to hear that, truly."

There was a lingering tension in the air, the unspoken words hung heavy between them.

Abby arrived carrying two cups of coffee. She glanced at Derek and then Hannah. Without saying a word, she set the coffee cups down on the table and sat down.

Hannah said, while grasping her coffee cup. "Well, Derek, I hope you find what you're looking for. As for me, I'm moving forward."

Forgetting about what he originally came into the coffee shop for, Derek left the coffee shop, his expression a mix of regret and longing. Hannah watched him jump into his father's company pickup truck. The sign on the side of the truck door stated: "Taylor Christmas Tree Farm." Abby and Hannah silently sipped their coffee.

*****

In the heart of Tennessee, winter wrapped its cold fingers around the small towns, painting them in hues of frost and the warm glow of holiday lights. The streets of downtown, bustling with the cheer of Christmastime, were alive with the magic of the season.

On the outskirts of Nashville, it wasn't a large house, but it was their childhood home. Abby and Hannah waited on the porch, breathing puffs of clouds into the chilly air as they knocked on the door. The door soon swung open, and a smiling face greeted them.

Hugging his two daughters, John said, "Abby and Hannah, it's so great you made it."

Hannah replied, with a tear rolling down her face, "It's nice to be home for Christmas."

Abby chimed in, "Besides, Mom made it sound important that we be here."

"Yeah, urgent even!" Hannah exclaimed. "What's that all about?"

John paused, then said solemnly, "Come inside so I can close the door." Then, with a barely noticeable chuckle, added, "I can't afford to warm up all of Tennessee."

With a suitcase in tow, Abby as the oldest crossed the threshold first, then Hannah, her guitar strap over one shoulder while towing her rolling suitcase.

John asked, while closing the door behind them, "So where's James?"

Abby remarked, "James and I were coming here for Christmas next year, like our every other year thing. But we told his parents that I had to be here this Christmas. James is going to his parents' house for a day." With a little sadness in her voice, she continues, "Then he has to go back to the big city for work."

"On Christmas?" John exclaimed.

"That's the price of being a big-city lawyer," Abby said with a shrug.

Hannah interrupted, "What's so urgent? I dropped everything to come down here."

"Ella has been waiting for you to arrive for days now." John quickly changed the subject with a nod toward the living room.

Their sister Ella, at ten years old, was the youngest of the Gerard girls. She sat silently in a chair, looking out the front window.

Hannah left her suitcase by the sofa and walked over to Ella. Ella smiled shyly as Hannah gave her a hug.

"Ella, I missed you," said Hannah, smiling.

Ella hugged her sister back but didn't say a word.

In the hallway, Abby asked in a lowered voice, "She's still not talking?"

"The doctor said that there's nothing physically wrong with her," John said with a tear in his eye. "It's called selective mutism, an anxiety disorder similar to PTSD, where a child stops talking. Maybe in time…"

Hannah walked back over to John and Abby.

Abby slowly shook her head. "You would think she would be over it by now. It's been six years."

Hannah remarked, "And a ton of expensive therapy."

"That's not the way it works, girls. She loved your grandma dearly. How would you have reacted if you were in her shoes?" John questioned.

Abby said, "Honestly, I'm not sure. I can't imagine being that little, all alone, watching someone die and you can't do anything about it."

Hannah looked determined. "I'm sure I would be traumatized too, but I would have talked through it."

John gently placed his hand on Hannah's shoulder. "You've always been great at talking through your feelings and putting them into songs, but Ella isn't like that. She's always been more reserved."

John's gaze lingered on Hannah and Abby, a tapestry of concern and unspoken truths etched across his features. The weight of his wife's illness, a secret guarded at her behest, lay heavy on his heart. Yet to his daughters, his words seemed to revolve around their youngest sister, Ella. He drew a slow, steadying breath. "God's timing isn't always as fast as we would like. All we can do is pray."

Hannah walked over to Ella and gave her another warm hug. "I remember when Mom brought you home from the hospital. I thought you were my own baby doll."

"Why don't you two get settled in," John said gently to his two daughters. He took his coat from the hall closet and put it on. "I have to go and pick up your mother."

"Where is Mom?" Abby asked.

John turned and left the house without responding.

Abby and Hannah glanced at each other in bewilderment. "Something is going on," Hannah said suspiciously.

"I guess we'll just have to wait until Mom gets home." Abby picked up her suitcase and headed toward her bedroom.

Chapter 3

Under the warm glow of the afternoon sun, John Gerard lingered patiently in the pickup zone outside Nashville General Hospital. His gaze was fixed on the entrance, awaiting his wife's appearance. Moments later, she emerged, in a wheelchair, her journey eased by the gentle hands of a nurse whose smile radiated warmth and comfort.

Grace, her voice tinged with a mix of annoyance and independence, asked, "Is the wheelchair really necessary?"

The nurse, adhering to the rules with a gentle firmness, replied, "It's hospital policy."

Grace, her spirit undimmed, protested lightly, "But I can walk perfectly fine."

Unfazed, the nurse continued her task, guiding Grace toward the pickup truck. John, ever the attentive husband, leaped from the driver's seat, his movements quick and fluid, to open the passenger door for her.

With a heartfelt "Thank you" directed at the nurse, Grace acknowledged the kindness she had been shown.

The nurse offered a parting smile before retreating, leaving John to tenderly assist his wife into the truck. He closed the door with care then settled himself into the driver's seat.

Breaking the silence, John's voice, soft and laced with concern, inquired, "So how did everything go?"

The question unraveled the composure Grace had held onto. Tears began to stream down her cheeks, a silent testament to the emotions she harbored. Sensing her need, John wrapped his arm around her, offering the solace of his presence.

*****

Abby left for her bedroom. When she opened her bedroom door, a small smile crossed her face. Her room was exactly how she left it. She sighed. "Mom's so sentimental."

Abby threw her suitcase on the bed and unzipped it. She shook out her clothes and put those that needed hangers in the closet. The other garments, she put in drawers. After finishing, she plopped on her bed and reached for her little pink princess telephone. She smirked with a little twinkle in her eye. "Nothing has changed."

She dialed a familiar number. "Hey, love."

"Hi, sweetheart," her husband, James, said with a sparkle in his voice.

Abby asked, "Did you tell your parents again how sorry I am that I can't be there for Christmas?"

"Of course." James took a breath. "They wanted more info about why, so I just said some kind of family emergency. Is it?"

"I still don't know what is going on. My dad is being very elusive." Abby sighed. "I guess I'll have to wait until my mom gets home."

"Call me when you find out," chuckled James. "There are many curious people here who want to know."

Abby laughed. "Count me as one of them."

James asked with concern, "How are you feeling?"

"I'm just a little tired from the flight. At least the morning sickness part is over."

"Call me later. Bye, love," James said then kissed the phone.

Abby kissed the phone and said, "Bye, darling."

*****

Across the hall, after Hannah had unpacked her small suitcase, she unzipped her guitar bag and removed her guitar.

Hannah, with guitar in hand, ambled to the living room. Sitting next to Ella, she strummed the guitar in the process of composing the song that had been growing in her heart for months.

Ella smiled, seemingly comforted by the gentle music.

"I've been working on a new song," Hannah said. "It's my Christmas present for Mom, but I'm at a loss for words. Maybe you can help me?" Hannah smiled at Ella. Ella smiled and scrunched up closer to her sister. Hannah strummed the guitar and hummed the lyrics she had while trying to think of better ones.

Hearing her parents' car pulling up in the driveway, Ella looked out the window. Hannah stopped playing her guitar as her eyes followed Ella's movement. Ella had a big smile on her face. "Abby!" shouted Hannah as she and Ella jumped up from the couch. "Mom's home!"

Abby bounded out of her bedroom and stood next to Hannah and Ella who were now waiting anxiously by the front door. The three looked like a jury awaiting the prime witness.

The front door opened and their mother entered, followed by their father. Abby and Hannah ran to their mother, hugging her warmly. Ella hugged her mother tightly, not wanting to let go.

Grace laughed. "I'm so happy to see you girls. Christmas just isn't the same without you." Hannah stepped back and quickly inquired, "Dad won't tell us what's going on."

"Yes, Mom, what's the emergency?" Abby asked, standing in front of her looking perplexed.

"Later," said Grace, slipping from Ella's embrace. "John, get the Kodak. I want a picture of the family by the fireplace."

Hannah handed her dad her cell phone. "Here, Dad, use my cellphone."

John smiled. "You know your mother wants physical pictures for her photo album."

Hannah shook her head as her dad walked down the hallway to fetch the old camera. "You know that I can print them from the digital photos."

As they were gathering by the fireplace, Abby whispered into Hannah's ear, "You can't teach an old dog new tricks."

John quickly returned and set the old 35mm camera on a tri-pod. After setting the timer, he stepped quickly over to the family. Standing next to his wife, he put an arm around her to steady her. The camera flashed.

Grace said, "I am going to start dinner." And quickly headed to the kitchen.

Hannah said with her hands on her hips, "Wait, aren't you going to tell us what's going on?"

As her mother disappeared into the kitchen, Abby remarked, "That's how you're going to leave us hanging?"

"Let your mother be," John said. "There will be plenty of time for explanations."

Abby sighed. Hannah pushed out a deep breath of frustration.

"While your mother is making dinner, I have a job for you girls," John said to Abby and Hannah. Hannah's head cocked to one side. "Job?"

John laughed. "A fun task. Don't worry, you'll enjoy it."

Abby and Hannah's brows furrowed. John laughed harder. "We need to put the ornaments on the Christmas tree and put up the decorations in the living room."

Ella smiled; she had been waiting to decorate.

Abby peered around the living room. "What Christmas tree?"

There was a knock on the door. John said, "That would be our Christmas tree."

John opened the door, and Derek came in carrying a seven-foot perfectly shaped tall Scotch Pine tree.

"What are you doing here?" Hannah snapped.

"Hannah, be nice," John said. "Derek's father gave us a huge discount on this tree."

Hannah gave Derek a stink eye. "But did Derek have to deliver it?"

"Hannah," John growled. "Why don't you girls get the Christmas decorations from the attic while Derek and I set up the tree?"

"Come on, Abby, let's go get the decorations." Hannah huffed as she walked away.

*****

Abby pulled the thick cord hanging at the end of the hallway, bringing down the staircase leading to the attic. Being the more adventurous of the two, Hannah went up first. Abby waited until Hannah was in the attic before joining her.

A dim light came to life when Hannah grabbed the dangling string and jerked it. Cardboard boxes were stacked neatly around the triangular-roofed attic.

"At least everything is clearly marked," Hannah said, looking at the neatly lettered boxes.

Abby laughed. "Dad and his labels."

"I remember him labeling our bicycles." Hannah chuckled.

Abby raised one eyebrow. "That was because you kept 'borrowing' my bicycle."

Hannah said with a sly grin, "In my defense, they WERE the same color."

Abby smiled in agreement, shaking her head playfully.

Hannah slid two cardboard boxes toward the staircase. "You go down first, and I'll hand you the boxes."

Once the boxes were safely on the hallway floor, they each took a box and carried them into the living room.

"Nice tree," Hannah said, admiring the seven-foot Christmas tree.

"Let's get to work," John said. "I want to get this tree decorated by the time your mother finishes cooking dinner."

Abby laughed. "No pressure."

"We'll have the whole room decorated by then," Hannah exclaimed, bending over and opening a box marked "tree decorations." "Mom's Christmas dinners are always a banquet to die for."

John's face paled at the word *die* and quickly turned his head toward the tree. "Derek, do you want to stay for dinner?"

Hannah gasped.

"Sure, Mr. G, I'll have to return the company truck, and then I'll be back," Derek said, smirking at Hannah.

When Derek left, Hannah said, "Why did you have to invite him to our family dinner?"

John placed his hands on his hips. "I don't know what's gotten into you, Hannah. You two grew up together. You two used to be inseparable."

"That was before we went to college." Hannah huffed.

*****

Abby unfolded the flaps of the second box, and Ella was there in a flash. Ella silently dug through the box and pulled out the red-and-white shelf elf.

Hannah glanced over. "That old elf is still around?"

"Petey," Abby said.

Hannah said, "That's right, Petey."

"I remember Mom putting him all over the house." Abby laughed. "That elf must be twenty years old by now."

Hannah doubled over laughing. "I remember when she put him in the tree, and the tree almost fell over when you tried to move him."

Ella silently clung to the little worn cloth elf and walked over to the fireplace and placed it on the mantle.

John whispered to Abby and Hannah, "Ella still loves that little guy. It makes her eyes light up when she finds it moved in the morning. Even though she knows Grace is doing it."

Abby sighed. "I love that about Mom. She keeps the magic of Christmas alive." Ella smiled; she was a mama's girl.

John said, "Let's get to work, or we'll never finish by suppertime."

Ella placed ornaments on the lower branches, Abby in the middle, and John placed his ornaments on the tallest branches. Hannah sat on the couch with her guitar, playing Christmas carols as they all sang along.

Hannah said gleefully, "Let's make this tree a masterpiece!"

John said playfully, "Every year, you say that. And why don't you come and help us, huh? We can't make it a masterpiece without you."

Abby laughed. "And every year, it becomes more magical, Dad."

Hannah said with a distant expression, "Magical, indeed." Hannah got up, grabbed an ornament, and placed it on the tree.

Ella walked over to the couch and thumbed through the Bible on the end table. Abby smiled as she held up a little glass ornament in the shape of a moose.

"I remember those!" Hannah said as she rooted through the box of ornaments. "Aha! I found it!"

Hannah held up a colorful glass ornament of a bear cub. They both held the ornaments up to the light.

"Mom bought these for us on our trip to North Pole, Alaska," Abby said, admiring her ornament.

"Where is Ella's ornament?" Hannah asked, stooping over and looking in the box. Hearing her name, Ella glanced up from the open Bible.

"Here it is!" exclaimed Hannah, holding up the shiny glass ornament. Hannah held the sled dog ornament in an outstretched arm, showing Ella. "Remember this, Ella?"

Ella smiled and nodded her head. Then she returned to flipping through the Bible pages. Abby and Hannah hung the ornaments on the tree branches.

Ella walked over to her dad and handed him the open Bible.

John smiled. "Thank you, Ella." John glanced down at the open page and said, "Good one, you remembered. Luke, chapter two."

Ella smiled.

Hannah and Abby smiled at Ella.

Hannah said, "Ella has always been great at reminding us of what Christmas is really about."

Abby said, "Yep, Jesus is the reason for the season. Thanks, Ella!"

Hannah held her breath and slipped out her cell phone. She quickly jotted down an idea that had just come to her.

John closed the Bible and said to Ella, "Let's put this down for now. You know we always read the story of Jesus's birth on Christmas morning." Ella nodded and took the Bible, placing it back on the end table.

The girls watched as John placed the sparkling star on top of the tree.

As they all stood back and admired the decorated tree, John said, "Good work, girls."

Hannah grabbed her guitar and softly played a Christmas song.

Abby said, "I miss Grandma's famous pies."

At the mention of Grandma, Hannah noticed Ella's countenance drop. Hannah laid down her guitar and gave Ella a comforting hug.

"I'm going to see if Mom needs any help in the kitchen," Abby said as she left the living room.

*****

Abby, her features reflecting both concern and the gentle glow of pregnancy, moved closer to her mother. "Do you need a hand with anything?"

Grace, steadfast in her task of preparing the turkey, offered a faint smile. "No, dear, I've got this under control."

But Abby, unable to shake a sense of unease, stood by her side. "Mom, what's this secret you and Dad have been guarding? It feels like there's something you're not telling us."

Grace paused, her hands stilling over the festive bird. The weight of her illness, a shadow only she bore, loomed in her mind. She had resolved to shield her children from this dark truth until after the holidays, longing to bask in their unburdened joy rather than drown in their sorrow.

"There's time for that later," she said softly, avoiding her daughter's probing gaze.

Abby persisted, her voice laced with earnestness. "I want to help, Mom. Really."

Grace met her daughter's eyes, seeing in them the inevitable support and strength that would emerge once her secret was revealed. Shaking off these thoughts, she directed Abby with a task to distract them both. "All right then. Could you open a couple of cans of cranberries?"

As Abby turned to the task, her intuition nudged at her. Her mother, usually the embodiment of cheerfulness and vitality, seemed subdued today. But respecting the unspoken boundaries, Abby remained quiet, her worries unvoiced.

*****

There was a knock at the front door. Ella peeked out the window and ran to open the door. Hannah, curious, also went to the door. Ella opened the door a little and smiled at Derek. Hannah, behind the door, came around and saw Derek. "Oh, it's you."

"I brought you this," Derek said, holding out a small present neatly wrapped.

Hannah took the present and said with the minimum politeness that she could muster, "Thanks." Still feeling the pain of their breakup, her next words were cold, and she said, "I didn't get you anything."

Derek, trying to be diplomatic, said, "That's understandable."

"Derek, come and help us finish decorating the room," John said from the living room.

"Right away, Mr. G," Derek said, walking away from Hannah and Ella. Ella closed the door while Hannah fumed.

Chapter 4

The Gerard family's kitchen, usually a beacon of warmth and laughter, was jolted by an explosion of crashing pots and pans.

"Help!" Abby screamed, her voice laced with panic. "Help! It's Mom!" her shouts echoed through the home.

Instantly, the family rushed into the kitchen. Grace lay among the fallen cookware, her face etched with confusion and pain. Abby stood nearby, her eyes wide with shock.

Little Ella, her eyes brimming with tears, sprinted to her mother and clung to Grace as if she were the only anchor in a stormy sea.

John, steady and composed, knelt beside his wife. "Grace, are you okay?" he asked, concern coloring his tone.

Hannah, her voice a soothing melody, knelt beside Ella. "Ella, let Mommy get up. It's okay. I've got you," she coaxed, trying to gently pry Ella away.

Derek, quietly supportive, reached out to help. "Let me see if she's hurt," he offered, his voice steady.

Grace, her voice faint but steady, reassured, "I'm okay, sweetie."

John and Derek carefully helped Grace to her feet, while Hannah finally managed to embrace Ella, her arms offering solace and security.

In the aftermath, John guided Grace out of the kitchen, his arm protectively around her. Abby and Derek began the task of cleaning up, their movements automatic.

*****

John gently ushered his beloved Grace to their bedroom, his voice tinged with tender concern, "You need to rest, love."

Grace, ever the resilient soul, protested weakly, "But dinner won't make itself."

"We'll take care of it," John reassured her with a soft insistence.

With a sigh of surrender, Grace allowed her weary body to find solace beneath the comforting sheets, her shoes left forgotten by the bedside.

John, with a loving touch, planted a gentle kiss on her forehead. "Rest now," he whispered.

"I love you," the frail whisper escaped Grace's lips, an affirmation of love, barely audible yet profound.

The cruel grip of her illness was evident in her fading strength.

John echoed her sentiments, his heart heavy with emotion. "I love you too. I'll be right back to check on you," he promised, casting a lingering, fraught glance at his wife. The weight of the secret they harbored about her illness—a burden they kept from their daughters—lay heavily between them. Grace's wish was to shield them from the truth, but John's heart ached with the opposite desire. He believed their daughters deserved to know, sooner rather than later, before time stole Grace away forever.

*****

Hannah, with Ella now calm, sat her little sister at the kitchen table. Derek stood in the hallway, not knowing what to say himself, shocked at Hannah's mother's illness. They were all silent, each lost in their own thoughts. Hannah left the kitchen.

In the hallway, Hannah stopped her father. "Dad, how's Mom?"

John sighed, a weariness in his voice. "She's resting now. How's Ella?"

Hannah's frustration was palpable. "She's calmed down. But, Dad, it's been six years. Why won't Ella talk?"

"It's hard," John admitted, his voice heavy with unspoken worries. "Your mom and I, we've tried everything. But sometimes…it's just not enough."

In the kitchen, a somber family meeting unfolded. John patted Ella on the head. "You okay, kiddo?"

Ella nodded slightly.

John, his usual resilience faltering, struggled to find the words. "Girls, there's something I need to tell you."

Abby, sensing the gravity in his voice, stepped closer. "Dad, what is it? You can tell us."

John's voice broke as he delivered the news. "Your mother… She has lung cancer. And it's serious."

The revelation hit like a tidal wave, leaving shock and disbelief in its wake. Ella, her small frame shaking, buried her face in her hands.

"How serious?" Hannah demanded. "There are treatments for that, right?"

John sighed. "It is way past treatment. We found out too late."

"How long?" Hannah asked.

John could barely get the words out. "The doctors say three months."

Abby, her hand instinctively on her belly, gasped. "But my baby… Mom won't get to see her granddaughter?"

John, tears streaming down his face, could only offer a heartbroken look. Hannah, her voice trembling, asked, "How long have you known?"

Abby's voice was a mixture of pain and anger. "Why didn't you tell us sooner? Have you gotten a second opinion?"

"We only found out a few weeks ago," John explained, his voice thick with emotion. "Your mother… She wanted one last Christmas without this hanging over us."

Abby, wiping her tears, looked around the kitchen, trying to find some semblance of normalcy. "I'll finish dinner," she said, her voice barely a whisper. Letting the water running from the faucet match the flow from her eyes, Abby faced the sink, hiding her deep emotions from the others.

Hannah smirked. "Yeah, right, you're going to make dinner?"

Abby turned, a couple of tear drops falling to the floor. She gave Hannah a dirty look. "Really, Hannah? At least I know how to cook. You can't even boil water."

Hannah, her eyes flashing with a mix of grief and disbelief, stormed out. "I need to call Travis," she muttered, her footsteps echoing her turmoil.

John, the paternal figure, gently nudges Derek, the twenty-three-year-old neighborhood kid who's been a part of the family since his toddler years, to assist in tidying the living room as they await dinner. The request serves as a subtle distraction from the heavy atmosphere, thick with concern over Grace's sickness.

Derek, deeply integrated into the family's fabric, is visibly shaken by this revelation. His response to John is tinged with a blend of respect and genuine distress, reflecting his close bond with the family. "Yes, sir, Mr. G," he says, his voice betraying the turmoil within him.

Meanwhile, Ella, the youngest family member, quietly retreated to her bedroom, her head bowed in a silent, introspective struggle with the news. Her departure underscored the individual way each member was processing unexpected and painful information.

As the family members dispersed, each lost in their thoughts, the kitchen remained silent. This stillness spoke volumes, serving as a poignant reminder of life's unpredictability and the enduring resilience of love that bound the family together.

In the living room, Derek, seeking to express his empathy and offer support, addressed John with a sincere offer of assistance. "Mr. G, I am so sorry about Mrs. G's illness," he said, his voice laden with concern.

John, acknowledging Derek's sentiment, responds with gratitude. "Thank you, Derek," he said, recognizing the young man's long-standing presence and contributions to their household.

"If there is anything you need, please let me know," Derek offered earnestly, his willingness to help reflecting his deep affection for the family.

John's reply, warm and appreciative, highlights Derek's integral role in their lives. "You have always been a great help around here, and we are grateful," he said. "In fact, you are like a permanent fixture around here."

Derek, comforted by these words, smiled and expressed his affection for the family. "I do what I can. You are like my second family," he admitted, his smile a small beacon of warmth in the somber setting.

John, seeking to lighten the mood, playfully nudges the conversation back to the task at hand. "Okay, with that, the living room isn't going to clean itself," he said goodheartedly, injecting a hint of normalcy into the strained atmosphere.

Derek, responding to John's cue, smiled and echoed his earlier response, a mix of respect and affection in his voice. "Yes, sir, Mr. G," he said, ready to assist, embodying the spirit of family and community support that resonated throughout the scene.

As Derek helped John clean up the living room, his thoughts went back to Hannah. Always Hannah. Nestled near the Gerard estate, the Taylor tree farm breathed life into countless childhood memories for Derek Taylor and Hannah Gerard. From the moment their toddling feet had wandered the earth, their friendship blossomed, as natural and enduring as the evergreens surrounding them. Within the verdant embrace of Derek's father's Christmas tree farm, they wove tales of adventure and mystery, while playing hide-and-seek amidst the whispering pines.

Their youth was a tapestry of idyllic moments spent beside the serene lake where they listened to the serenade of frogs under a moon-kissed sky, the water mirroring the celestial ballet above. This shared wonder seemed a prelude to an inevitable future, one their families envisioned with quiet smiles—a union of hearts and lives in matrimony, a dream of shared tomorrows.

As they had ventured through the gates of academia, their bond deepened, an unspoken promise kindling between them. By their third year of college an unofficial engagement bound them to a seemingly predestined future. Yet when their paths diverged, the shockwave of their separation reverberated not just through their own hearts but also through the families that had dreamt of their union. It was a fracture in the perfect image of what could have been, leaving Hannah especially adrift in a sea of unfulfilled promises.

*****

Hannah plopped on her bed next to her guitar. She looked at her guitar and ran her fingers down the strings, then pushed it away out of frustration and sadness. She took a deep breath, grabbed her phone from her nightstand, and called Travis.

Travis answered the phone, "Howdy, babe."

Hannah said, "We have to change the wedding date."

"Uh, hold on, darlin'." Travis covered the phone with his hand and, in a muffled voice, shouted, "Yeah, put the Palomino in stall three." Uncovering the telephone, he continued, "What's going on?"

Hannah sounded desperate. "My mom's dying. She must be at the wedding, Travis. We have to move the date."

"Whoa, whoa, whoa, slow down. Let's think this through. The Grange Hall is booked a year in advance. We can't reschedule that."

"Then we're going to have to move the ceremony somewhere else. I don't even know if my mom will be able to travel. Maybe we just have it in Tennessee?"

In the background, coming from Travis's phone, a worker said, "Travis, we need your help getting Blazer rounded up."

Travis said, "Darling, it's just not a good time right now. I'm sorry about your mom. Call me later, okay?"

As Travis hung up the phone, Hannah stared at her phone in disbelief.

Hannah sat on her bed, picked up her guitar, and began strumming it, trying to find the right chords and lyrics to the song for her mother that had been swimming around in her head. She sang softly, "We're home for the holidays, making memories…" She began to cry. "Making memories? Today was an awful memory." She continued strumming her guitar and singing in almost a whisper. "Making memories we'll remember when we're old…" She sat down her guitar and laid back on her bed. "I just can't do this right now. When we're old?" She wiped a tear that ran down her cheek. "Mom isn't that old." She closed her eyes tight. "Lord, please heal our mom." As the prayer lingered in her mind, she stood up, shaking, and headed toward the kitchen.

*****

Abby, pleased at her attempt at finishing up dinner, set the oven's timer and then left for her bedroom.

She entered her bedroom and went right to the princess phone and dialed her husband.

Abby's voice trembled, and she tried, to no avail, to hold back her tears. "I can't believe this is happening."

James said with concern, "I feel for you, honey. This news is devastating."

Abby whimpered in a quivery voice, "It doesn't feel like Christmas anymore."

"It's not over yet. Miracles do happen," James said.

"I don't even want to open my presents. I don't want to see smiling faces. I just want to crawl up into a hole and hide forever."

"What do you think your mother would want?" James said sternly. "She invited you all there because she loves you."

Abby sobbed. "What am I supposed to do? I can't change the way I feel."

"Make this the happiest, most memorable Christmas ever. After all, this might be your last Christmas with your mother."

Abby went silent.

"Abby?" James asked with concern in his voice.

"I'm here. You're right. I owe it to my mother to keep my chin up. If not for me, then for the rest of the family."

"That's my girl," said James proudly. "Call me later. Love you."

"Love you too."

*****

Ella sat at her little desk in her bedroom, staring at the painting she had made of her family. She had painted it as a Christmas present for her family. Under each figure were their names: Dad, Mom, Abby, Hannah, and herself. Tears welled up in her eyes as she used her fine brush to draw her grandmother in the clouds. Her mind went back to that fateful day of the tragedy.

*****

Sunlight had filtered through lace curtains, painting a warm scene of innocence. Ella, a four-year-old bundle of energy and curiosity, engaged in imaginative play. Her grandmother, a source of comfort, watched her from her armchair.

Grandmother said, "Ella, sweetheart, can you make your dolls have a tea party?"

Ella's laughter danced in the air as she arranged her dolls.

Ella said gleefully, "Okay, Grandma! Look, they're having tea!"

Suddenly, her grandmother's face twisted in pain. She clutched her chest, collapsing to the floor. Ella's laughter turned into terror.

Ella, grabbing her grandmother's hand, shouting in horror, "Grandma! No, no, no! What's wrong?"

Ella's heart raced as she watched her grandmother struggle. She was too young to understand the gravity of the situation. Desperate, she tried to shake her grandmother awake.

Ella whispered, voice trembling, "Wake up, Grandma. Please wake up."

Hours passed, and the room was now dimmer as the sun began its descent. Ella was no longer playing. She sat beside her grandmother's lifeless form, eyes wide with terror. Her world was a labyrinth of fear. Ella's parents hadn't returned home yet, leaving her alone in the abyss of the unknown. The silence in the room was oppressive, a testament to Ella's isolation. Time seemed to stretch on endlessly.

As twilight blanketed the room, Ella's fear deepened. She curled up beside her grandmother, clutching her icy cold hand. The air was heavy with grief. Ella's parents finally arrived home, the front door creaking open.

Grace shouted, "Ella, we're home!"

They entered the living room, their voices echoing in the quiet house. Horror washed over them as they found Ella sitting beside her deceased grandmother.

John said, horrified, "Ella, sweetheart, what happened?"

Ella's eyes met her parents, her innocence shattered. She stared at them in silence, unable to utter a single word. The trauma had stolen her voice.

John knelt and felt for a pulse on his mother's neck. Tears welled up. "She's gone."

"I'll call 911," Grace said, the steadier of them.

After the police had left and the coroner had taken away their beloved grandmother, the room was now enveloped in darkness, save for a single dim lamp. In the soft glow of the solitary lamp, Ella's parents cradled her in a tender embrace. They shared a silent mourning, their collective grief uniting them in this moment of sorrow. Ella's gaze bore the weight of what she had seen, her voice stilled by the shock.

Outside her room, under the muted hall light, Grace turned to John with concern in her eyes. "How are you holding up?" she asked gently.

John's voice trembled slightly. "I'm reeling from what's happened to Ella. Could this just be a temporary shock?"

Grace reached for his hand, her touch warm and reassuring. "I'm not talking about Ella right now. How are you, with your mother's passing?"

A heavy sigh escaped John. "It's like there's a void inside me."

Grace's voice softened. "Your mother's death marks the end of an era. Our children have lost their last grandparent."

John's shoulders slumped, the weight of the world seemingly on them. "It feels like everything is on me now."

Grace stood closer, her eyes filled with unwavering support. "Not just you, us. We're in this life journey together, as partners."

In a moment of shared understanding, John leaned in and kissed Grace. John, followed by Grace, carried the now-sleepy Ella to her bed. And soon, hand in hand, they walked toward their bedroom, a symbol of their unbreakable bond in the face of life's trials.

*****

Ella's mind came back to the present. She stared at the drawing she had just completed. It was to be a present for the family. Anger overwhelmed her. With tears streaming down her face, she took out one of her artist brushes. After dipping the brush into black acrylic paint, she smeared the black paint all over the picture. She then slid down to the floor weeping.

Chapter 5

Derek continued helping John clean up the living room. They were alone; the three sisters were in their bedrooms dealing with the tragic news of their mother's sickness. Grace was resting in bed. As they were quietly finishing, John told Derek, "I'll be right back. I'm going to check on Grace."

In the dim light of their bedroom, John slid onto the bed and held her closely. The steady rise and fall of her breath was a painful reminder of the news that had shattered their world. The walls, adorned with family photos, seemed to echo with silent grief. John looked down upon his dear wife; thirty years they had devoted to each other. Her face is a little more wrinkled now but is still just as lovely as when he first met her. His thoughts went back to when he had first laid eyes on her.

*****

Grace, an eighteen-year-old with a heart full of faith and a deep devotion to the Lord, had embarked on a life-changing journey when she attended a Christian summer camp. Little did she know that this experience would introduce her to John, a young man who shared her unwavering belief and would become a significant part of her life. John, only two years her senior, stood out as a strong Christian figure and even held the role of a youth leader at the camp. His passion for serving the Lord mirrored Grace's, and his strong character was matched by his gentle spirit.

During the camp, John couldn't help but notice Grace's devotion and kind heart, which was complemented by her striking beauty. As their paths crossed more frequently, they found themselves gravitating toward one another during John's off-hours. Their conversations flowed effortlessly, and the more time they spent together, the deeper their connection grew. It didn't take long for the two of them to realize that they were falling in love, their shared faith acting as a powerful bond that brought them closer with each passing day.

In the blink of an eye, six months had passed since they first met at the summer camp, and they both knew that what they had was something special. Their love was not only deeply rooted in their faith but also in the way they complemented and supported each other. With unwavering conviction and a sense of divine guidance, they had made the decision to start a new chapter together. In a beautiful ceremony surrounded by family and friends they were married, that was thirty years ago.

In the present, in the dim light of the bedroom, John held Grace tighter. He said in a whisper, "I told them."

"Oh no, the girls?" Grace's eyes widened. "How did they react?"

"Of course, they all were shocked. We'll have to give them a little time to process the news."

"John," Grace's voice was a whisper, fragile like autumn leaves. "I'm scared. Not for me. I know where I am going, but I'm so scared of not being here for our girls."

He tightened his hold, his heart aching. "I know, love. I know."

"I won't see Abby's baby or be there for Hannah's wedding." Her words tumbled out, steeped in sorrow. "And Ella… How will she cope without me?"

John's eyes moistened. "We'll find a way, Grace. We always do."

"But how? How do you prepare for a goodbye you're not ready for?" Grace buried her face in his chest.

John had no answers, only the warmth of his embrace. "We'll do it together. We'll make sure the girls are ready. Abby is strong, and James is there for her. Hannah's got that spark in her eyes. She'll make it through. And Ella…Ella will find her voice again, I promise."

"I won't be here to see any of it." Grace's voice broke, and a tear slid down her cheek.

John brushed it away gently. "Then I'll make sure they remember you. Every day. In every way."

Grace looked up, her eyes reflecting a lifetime of love and fear. "Promise me, John. Promise me you'll help them remember."

"I promise, Grace. I promise." He pulled her closer, their hearts beating in a melancholic rhythm.

In the quiet of their sanctuary, unspoken words filled the air, weaving a tapestry of love, loss, and undying hope.

And in that moment, they understood that some promises, the most important ones, were made not just in words but in the unyielding strength of two hearts facing the unknown together.

*****

Hannah needed time to think. Her mother's situation had turned her world upside down, and she felt lost in a sea of emotions. She ran to the front door, her steps quick and urgent, and stepped outside. The evening air was cool and crisp, a stark contrast to the turmoil raging inside her.

Derek, seeing the distraught look on her face, rushed outside, his own heart pounding with a mix of concern and unspoken feelings. He found Hannah sitting on the front porch swing, her gaze distant, lost in thoughts a million miles away. He hesitated then approached her.

"I'm sorry about your mom," Derek said softly, breaking the silence between them.

Hannah gave a slight nod, her eyes glistening as she held back tears. She looked away, trying to hide her vulnerability. "Thank you. It's just…it's all so overwhelming."

Derek sat down beside her, the old swing creaking under their weight. He noticed her shiver in the cold night air. He took off his jacket and gently draped it around her shoulders. "You don't have to go through this alone," he offered quietly.

They sat in silence, each lost in their own thoughts. The night seemed to hold its breath, waiting for what would come next.

After a long pause, Hannah's voice, fragile and filled with emotion, broke the stillness. "You broke my heart. When you left, I felt like my world ended."

Derek's expression was one of pain and regret. "I know, and I'm so sorry. I was confused as to what was really important to me, to us. I didn't realize how much I was hurting you."

Hannah pulled her hand away as Derek reached for it, her emotions a tumultuous storm. "Derek, I'm engaged now," she said, her voice a whisper of the conflict within her.

Derek retracted his hand, as if burned. The words hit him hard, a painful reminder of what he had lost. "I should go," he said, his voice strained with the effort of holding back his emotions.

As Derek turned to leave, another tear escaped Hannah's eyes. She bowed her head, staring at the engagement ring that symbolized a commitment yet felt like a shackle. "Wait," she called out softly, her voice trembling. Hannah held out his jacket.

Derek stopped, turning back to her, a glimmer of hope in his eyes. He took the jacket and slipped it on.

"Why did you come back?" Hannah asked, her voice a mix of longing and despair.

"To Nashville?" Derek walked back to her, his expression earnest. "I came back for you. I realized I couldn't run from what I feel for you. But I see now it's too late."

Hannah met his eyes, her heart torn between the past and her present. "It's not just about us anymore. I have someone else to think about now."

"I'm going to go." Derek nodded, the pain evident in his eyes. "Tell your dad thanks for the dinner invite, but I have to leave."

He slowly walked to his car, each step heavy with the weight of what might have been. Hannah watched him drive away, the taillights disappearing into the night. She sat there, twisting her engagement ring around her finger, a symbol of her commitment but also of the choices that lay ahead.

*****

Grace stepped out of her bedroom, down the hallway, and weakly stepped into the living room. The living room was a montage of tense anticipation that dissolved as Grace sat down on one of the two recliners. Her face was a canvas of mixed emotions.

Abby, the eldest daughter, stood up immediately, cradling her pregnant belly protectively.

"Mom, how…how am I supposed to go through this without you?" Abby's voice quivered with fear and sorrow. "You might not be here to meet your grandchild."

Grace approached her, eyes filled with a mixture of sadness and love. "Abby, my dear," she said softly, "I will be there in every way that counts. In your heart, in your child's laughter. Always."

Hannah and Ella, the younger daughters, moved in closer, their actions speaking volumes in the silence. They wrapped their arms around Grace, each seeking and giving comfort without words.

Hannah finally broke the silence, her voice low but clear. "We'll make sure your grandchild knows about you, Mom. Every day, they'll know how amazing you are."

John, Grace's husband, stood a little apart, observing the scene with a mix of grief and pride. "Look at this, Grace. This is the love you've built," he said, his voice a steady anchor in the storm of emotions.

Surrounded by her family, Grace found herself enveloped in a cocoon of love and support, each member echoing their commitment and affection in the face of the challenging times ahead.

"Time to eat!" Grace announced with a playful grin, glancing toward Abby. "And witness the culinary magic Abby has whipped up from my humble beginnings."

Hannah leaned in with a mischievous smile. "Hear that, Abby? You've turned Mom's dinner into a gourmet feast. The pressure's on!"

Abby rolled her eyes playfully. "Oh, please, I just added a pinch of this and a dash of that. Don't make it a Broadway show!"

Hannah chuckled. "Well, let's dig in and see if Abby's 'pinch and dash' deserves a standing ovation."

*****

The Gerard family sat in a somber silence around the Christmas dinner table, a stark contrast to their usual lively gatherings. Grace, pale but smiling, caught the eyes of each of her daughters, her gaze lingering with a silent message of love.

Abby glanced at Hannah, breaking the silence. "This feels so strange, doesn't it? Christmas without laughter…"

Hannah nodded, her voice soft. "Yeah."

Ella left the table and returned holding the family Bible, extending it toward her father. Her eyes were earnest, pleading.

John looked at her, puzzled. "Ella, sweetheart, we'll read it tomorrow, remember?"

Ella, insistent, opened the Bible and pointed to a verse. John, understanding her silent request, read it aloud. "'Do not be anxious about anything, but in everything by prayer and supplication with thanksgiving let your requests be made known to God. And the peace of God, which surpasses all understanding, will guard your hearts and your minds in Christ Jesus' (Philippians 4:6–7)."

Abby's voice trembled as she reached for Grace's hand. "Dad, Ella's right. We should pray and believe He will give us healing and peace."

Hannah's voice carried a mix of sarcasm and hope. "Pray for a Christmas miracle, huh?"

Ella's smile was a beacon of hope. She took her father's hand then reached for Hannah's. Hannah, a little reluctantly, joined hands with Abby, who completed the circle with Grace.

John, his voice filled with emotion, led them in prayer. "Dear Lord, we ask for healing for Grace, for Ella, and for our family. Bring us peace and strength. Amen."

As they finished, the mood lightened. John, with a playful nudge, asked, "So who's going to pass me the rolls?"

Hannah smirked. "The rolls are probably the only thing that Abby didn't touch."

Abby frowned and playfully threw a roll at Hannah.

Their laughter, though subdued, filled the room with a warmth that had been absent since the news of their mother's sickness had shocked them. It was different this year, but the bond of the family felt stronger.

"Thank you, Abby," said Grace as they finished dinner. "Your pinch of this and a dash of that worked. Good job."

Hannah smirked. "Well, at least we know now that James won't be starving."

Abby raised her eyebrows and laughed.

John could see that Grace's strength waned. John stood up, concern etched on his face. "Let's let your mom rest. We all need to be fresh for tomorrow."

Abby and Hannah quickly agreed to clear the table. "We've got this," Abby said with a reassuring smile.

"We're going to bed." John said. "After you finish with the dishes, make sure everything is turned off."

Abby said, "I'll make sure the front door is locked and everything is put away."

John gently led Grace to their bedroom. Ella moved with a quiet grace, her steps echoing a newfound hope as she carefully placed the Bible back in the living room. She then slipped into her bedroom.

Abby and Hannah stood side by side at the sink, the remnants of dinner waiting patiently. The clatter of dishes punctuated the comfortable silence until Hannah broke it with a determined smile. "I'll wash, you dry."

Abby, her brows raised in playful defiance, retorted, "No way, Hannah. Ugh, you always leave something on the dishes."

Hannah, leaning against the counter with her arms crossed, shot back, "But drying takes so long."

"Not if you keep up," Abby countered, her tone light but firm.

A challenge sparkled in Hannah's eyes as she extended her hand. "Rock, paper, scissors?"

Abby's smirk was full of mischief. "You're on."

Their hands flew in a flurry of playful competition. Abby won the first round. Hannah's face lit up with hopeful excitement. "Two out of three?"

The sisters giggled, the tension of the day easing with each laugh. Abby triumphed again. "Three out of five?" Hannah asked, her voice tinged with hopeful persistence.

Abby, shaking her head with a victorious grin, tossed the kitchen towel at Hannah. "No, I won fair and square."

Hannah, with a shrug of resignation, accepted her fate, her smile never fading.

In the bedroom, John gently helped Grace to bed, his concern for her evident in his every careful movement. "Rest. You'll need your strength for tomorrow," he said softly, his voice a comforting blanket in the quiet room. Grace's eyes met his, gratitude and love mingling in her weary gaze. She nodded, her strength waning, but her spirit bolstered by the love that filled the room. John put on his pajamas and crawled into bed. He then reached over and turned off the light.

Chapter 6

The house was dark as the Gerard family slumbered. At midnight, Hannah, with her guitar in her hand and restless from a night of troubled thoughts, tiptoed to Ella's bedroom. Hannah listened at the door and heard soft sobbing. She softly tapped on the door while opening the door quietly.

Inside, the bedroom was a sanctuary of youthful innocence and creativity. Yet the stark black streaks across Ella's latest painting spoke of the grief consuming the young girl. Ella glanced up. She was sitting on the floor, her eyes puffy from crying throughout the night. Hannah's heart broke seeing her little sister this way. Hannah knelt beside Ella and wrapped her arms around her.

Hannah said, "I know it hurts. It's okay to feel hurt." Hannah glanced at the smeared painting. "And a little anger."

Ella looked down, unable to hold back her tears. Hannah said, "I don't want to lose her either." Ella, teary eyed, pointed to her chest.

Hannah said, "I hurt in there too."

Ella snuggled into Hannah's chest. Hannah and Ella cried, entwined in each other's arms. Ella's heart broke seeing her sister in pain. Hannah had always been there for her, from a scraped knee to her first bicycle ride. Hannah was always her encourager. Seeing Hannah weeping hurt Ella to the core. Ella clasped their hands together in prayer.

Words of comfort and shared sorrow passed between them, their bond strengthening in the face of impending loss. Hannah's prayer was a whisper of hope in the quiet room, a plea for a miracle they both desperately needed.

Ella's response, a small smile and a simple gesture pointing to her heart, spoke louder than any words. It was a moment of pure connection, a reminder that amid pain, the love of family endures.

Hannah smiled at her sister, remembering how Ella had first come into the world—a surprise to her parents but an overwhelming joy to Hannah. Hannah's excitement had bubbled over when she first held tiny Ella in her arms. At thirteen, Hannah was no longer a child, yet not quite an adult; and this new role of big sister bridged that gap perfectly. She would watch, wide-eyed, as her mother gently showed her how to cradle Ella's head, whispering stories of her own childhood and the bond of sisters.

In the hush of late nights, Hannah would tiptoe into Ella's nursery, the moon casting a soft glow over the crib. She'd reach out, brushing her finger against Ella's tiny, curled hand, marveling at the softness of her skin. When Ella would fuss, Hannah was there, humming melodies that danced between the walls and soothing her back to sleep.

As Ella grew, Hannah was her guardian and guide. She'd hold Ella's hands, helping her take those wobbly first steps, her heart swelling with pride at each tiny milestone. They'd spend afternoons in the garden, Hannah teaching Ella the names of flowers, their laughter mingling with the rustle of leaves.

Their bond was a tapestry of moments—the impromptu kitchen dance parties, the quiet afternoons reading side by side, the shared secrets whispered under starry skies. Ella's first word was a bubbly "Hannah," spoken with a gummy smile that lit up the room.

It was Hannah who eased her fears, weaving stories of magical adventures that awaited her. And as Ella listened, her eyes wide and sparkling, she'd clutch Hannah's hand, finding courage in her sister's presence.

As they grew, their bond only deepened. Hannah was Ella's confidante, her role model, the one who understood her unspoken thoughts. And for Hannah, Ella was a reminder of innocence, a burst of joy in the mundane, a connection to a part of her heart she never knew existed. Their love was a unique blend of sisterly affection and maternal care, a bond that held strong through the trials and triumphs of life.

As Hannah navigated the turbulent waters of adolescence, a shadow fell over her life with the tragic passing of their beloved grandmother. This loss, profound and piercing, struck Ella particularly hard. In the wake of this sorrow, Ella found herself engulfed in silence; she lost her voice, a manifestation of her deep grief.

For Hannah, watching Ella retreat into this silent world was heart-wrenching. She remembered the times when Ella's laughter was a constant melody in their home, and now the silence felt heavy, a palpable presence that filled every corner.

Hannah had confided in Ella, sharing her day-to-day experiences, her hopes, and her fears, just as they always had. She would sit by Ella's side, talking, sometimes reading aloud, hoping that the familiar cadence of her voice might offer comfort. In these moments, Ella's eyes would light up, a testament to the understanding and love that still flowed freely between them.

The sisters developed their own language of silent communication: a look, a touch, a smile—each a word in their unspoken conversations. Hannah held onto the hope that one day, Ella's voice would return, that once again, she would hear her sister speak. She had prayed for it in the quiet of the night, a whispered wish to the Lord.

Now at midnight, still sitting on the floor on this Christmas Eve, they found comfort in their embrace on the floor at the end of Ella's bed. Hannah's eyes were wet with tears. And although she tried to comfort her little sister, her grief was hard to hide. Ella found herself navigating through the uncharted waters of vulnerability, her heart aching as she witnessed Hannah, her rock, crumble under the weight of their mother's illness.

The sight of Hannah's tears shattered the illusion of invincibility that she had always associated with her older sister. Ella's soul was stirred by a mixture of fear, love, and a fierce desire to restore the light in Hannah's eyes. Hannah had always been her encourager, but now that fading strength scared her deeply. She wanted to do something to help Hannah. Ella pointed to Hannah's guitar.

In the stillness of Ella's room, Hannah picked up her guitar. The strings vibrated under her fingers, a familiar comfort. She began to sing the song she had been writing for their mother, her voice a blend of love and sadness.

Then a miracle unfolded. Ella's voice, silent for so long, joined Hannah's in a delicate harmony. It was a moment suspended in time, a healing balm for their wounded hearts. The song, a testament to their love for their mother, was also a bridge reconnecting Ella to the world she had retreated from.

Hannah was overwhelmed with joy. Ella smiled as she had found a way to bring joy back to her sister. Hannah grabbed Ella's hand, and they both rushed to share this miraculous turn with the rest of the family.

"Come here, everyone!" Hannah shouted down the hallway. "It's a miracle, a Christmas miracle!"

John and Grace came out of their bedroom. John, stretching and wiping his eyes, asked, "What's all the shouting all about?"

Ella smiled. She rushed to her mother and said, "Mommy."

Grace, overwhelmed, her knees weakening, dropped to the floor. John quickly held onto Grace's arm, softening her fall. Grace hugged Ella, rocking her in her arms. "My little Ella."

John's drowsiness evaporated in an instant. "Thank You, Jesus."

Abby came out of her bedroom, yawning, and said, "What is going on?"

Ella, still in their mother's embrace, said, "Abby."

Abby fell back against the hallway wall with eyes widened. She said, "Ella? You can speak? How? What happened?"

"It's an answer to prayer!" Hannah shouted.

"Indeed," John said, grinning, patting Ella on the head, and placing his arm around Grace. He glanced down at Grace. Their eyes met. "Maybe this will just be the first of many miracles."

The house, once shrouded in sorrow, now echoed with cheers and tears of happiness. It was a moment of profound change, a glimmer of light in the darkness. John, standing by his wife Grace's side—his face a canvas of mixed emotions—glanced around the hallway filled with his family.

Grace, frail but with a new spark in her eyes, leaned back against the wall, absorbing the joyous atmosphere. Her voice, though weak, carried the weight of their shared journey. "Yes, it really has been a good night." She then turned to John. "Get the Kodak."

"Grace," John protested. "It's midnight. We can take pictures tomorrow."

"No," Grace said as firmly as she could in her weakened state. "We need to preserve these moments when they happen."

John sighed; this was against his better judgment, but after one glance at his wife's pleading eyes, he rushed off and retrieved the camera from their bedroom.

He set the tripod in the hallway. He watched his wife leaning against the wall, looking exhausted, and quickly said, "Everyone gather around your mother."

The girls surrounded their mother. John set the timer and stepped quickly over to the wall. The camera flashed.

John, ever the pragmatic, tempered the joy with concern. "Grace, you really do need your rest," he said, his voice tinged with gentle firmness. Grace slowly nodded her head and allowed John to guide her to her bed.

Abby—the eldest daughter—her hand resting on her pregnant belly, stifled a yawn and smiled. "Yes, tomorrow is Christmas!" Her eyes sparkled with the excitement of the holiday and the happiness for her sister, little Ella.

Hannah chimed in with a playful tone. "Yeah, Ella, you surely want to see what Santa brought you." Her eyes danced with unspoken jokes and shared secrets.

Ella—the youngest—who had just found her voice again after years, rolled her eyes playfully. She knew Santa Claus wasn't real, but she played along for Hannah's sake. "Yes, I can't wait to see what he brought me." Her voice, still a bit quavering, was like music to her family's ears.

The room was filled with a new energy, a sense of hope and renewal. Each member of the family, from Grace fighting her illness to young Ella rediscovering her voice, was touched by the magic of the moment.

John, the anchor of the family, coughed, signaling the end of the night. He peeked out his bedroom door. "Good night, everyone," he said, his voice filled with gratitude and love.

As John crawled into bed, Grace whispered, "Yes, it really has been a good night." Her whisper lingered in the air.

The girls retreated to their rooms, hearts full, carrying with them the joy and miracles of the night.

Chapter 7

With the joy of hearing Ella's beautiful voice, the family gathered at the table as Abby and Hannah prepared their traditional Christmas breakfast. They reached out to hold hands, and John gave thanks for their time together, Ella's miracle, and the hope for Grace's healing. Their excitement couldn't be contained, and voices, especially Ella's, rang throughout the house.

In the din of excitement, Ella squealed, "Presents!" And everyone, as if on some silent command, slowly stood up and turned toward the beautifully decorated Christmas tree. Each eyeing the colorful wrapping paper on the stacks of presents. Abby, being the eldest, took over and started reading each label and handing the presents out. In minutes, wrapping paper was everywhere, some torn, some neatly folded, or just scattered on the floor. Leftover food on plates from breakfast was scattered around as well. And of course, Grace's old Kodak camera, which had plenty of use this morning, sat by her side.

There was a knock at the door. Ella rushed to answer it, and Hannah was on her heels. Ella opened the door, blocking Hannah from seeing who it was.

Derek, holding a wrapped present, said, "Hi, Ella."

"Hi, Derek," Ella said with a smile.

Derek's eyes widened as he took a step backward. "Ella? You can speak?"

Hannah came around the door. "Yes, she can. Now what do you want?"

"When did this happen? It's a miracle!" Derek said his mouth agape.

"Last night," Ella said, her eyes sparkling.

Hannah put her hands on her hips. "Yes, yes, a Christmas miracle. What are you doing here?"

"Hannah who is at the door?" John shouted from the living room.

"Derek," Ella answered.

"Well, let him in. We can't afford to heat up all of Tennessee."

Derek gave Hannah a self-assured wink as he came in. Hannah huffed as she followed him.

"Mr. G, Mrs. G," Derek said as he entered the living room. "My mom and dad got this for you." Derek thrust out a nicely decorated package.

John reached out and gave the present to Grace to unwrap. Grace said, "Tell your parents thank you."

Derek stepped over to Grace and held her hand. "I'm so sorry to hear about your illness."

Grace placed her other hand over his. "Thank you, Derek."

"Mrs. G, you've made such an impact on all of us. We're here for you, always," Derek said, his voice laced with heartfelt emotion.

John crawled under the tree and reached in and retrieved two presents. He handed them to Derek.

"One is for you, and one is for your parents."

"Thank you," Derek said. "Sorry I had to miss dinner yesterday."

John said, "Why don't you stay awhile and open your present?"

Derek sat on the couch next to Hannah. Hannah clutched her guitar and inched away.

Derek unwrapped his present, a new electronic tablet, and exclaimed, "Wow, thank you! You shouldn't have."

"Yeah, you shouldn't have," Hannah said sarcastically, glancing at her opened present—also an electronic tablet.

"We bought one for each of you," Grace said with a smile.

Hannah rolled her eyes. "Wonderful."

Ella, sitting on the floor at Hannah's feet, looked up to her and said, "When are you going to give Mom your present for her?"

Hannah smiled at Ella. She placed her guitar in her hands, ready to play, and said, "I wrote this song for you, Mom." Hannah began strumming her guitar and sang. She finished the song with the chorus, "Oh, Mama, your love's a song that lingers on. Through the highs and lows, it makes me strong. In your prayers, I find answers I may never get. Sometimes God says yes, no, or not yet."

Grace's warm smile was all the thank-you that Hannah needed.

"That was beautiful," Derek said. "I always said that you have the voice of an angel."

Hannah blushed. Ella went over and snuggled on her mother's lap. Abby and John started to clear the dishes and the wrapping paper on the floor.

Derek said in a low voice, "Remember in college when we ran out of gas out in the middle of nowhere?"

Hannah shook her head slowly. "Yeah, I remember it was in that old clunker of yours. Your phone was dead, and I had left mine in the dorm."

"We were lost in the middle of tall wheat and cow pastures in the dark, no streetlights out there. Then we heard that cow mooing behind us next to the fence."

Hannah gave a faint smile. "I almost jumped out of my skin."

Derek continued remembering. "You took your guitar out of the car and started to sing. Your music could soothe the wild beast."

Hannah elbowed him playfully. "And you sang so off-key I thought you were going to scare the cows."

"And finally, some farmer came by and gave us some gas for my car." Derek gave her a wink and a warm smile. "We have had some good times, haven't we?"

Hannah had to admit that they did have a lifetime of fun together.

Derek bent down, retrieving something from the floor. "You forgot this," he said, extending the small, neatly wrapped package that he had given to Hannah the day before.

With a hesitant hand, Hannah took the gift from Derek's grasp. The wrapping paper crinkled and tore under her fingers, revealing a small box. She opened it and gasped softly. Inside were delicate silver earrings, each shaped like a tiny frog. Memories flooded back—those endless summer nights by the lake, the chorus of frogs serenading them. Her eyes shimmered with unshed tears as she whispered, "Thank you, Derek."

Derek watched her, his expression a mix of hope and heartache. "Do they…remind you?"

Hannah nodded, clutching the earrings like a lifeline to the past. "They do. You always remembered the smallest details, the happiest moments…" Her voice trailed off, a storm of emotions swirling in her eyes.

"I wanted to give you something that meant…us. Our friendship," Derek confessed, his voice barely above a whisper.

Grace and John watched Hannah and Derek, tentative but clearly drawn to each other. Grace glanced at John from across the room, her eyes sparkling with a mix of hope and mischief. In that brief, silent exchange, volumes were spoken without a word being uttered. It was a look they had shared many times over the years, one that spoke of unspoken agreements and shared desires.

John, understanding immediately, returned her gaze with a subtle nod. His eyes, always so expressive, conveyed a depth of emotion. At that moment, they were both parents and partners in crime, united in their silent wish for their daughter's happiness. They didn't need words to understand each other's thoughts: both were thrilled at the prospect of Hannah and Derek rekindling their relationship, yet they had wisely chosen to stay out of it.

Hannah stood up abruptly, the moment overwhelming her. "I—I need to call Travis," she stuttered, avoiding Derek's gaze. Her heart was a battlefield of past and present.

Derek's face fell, a silent ache in his eyes. As she left the room, guitar in hand, he sat, lost in his longing, the ghost of their past lingering in the air. "I still love you, Hannah," he whispered, knowing his words would never reach her.

*****

Hannah laid on her bed and dialed the telephone.

"Hello?" her cousin Francine answered,

"Hi, Fran, I got good news and bad news," Hannah said. "It's Christmas time. Tell me the good news first."

"Ella's talking again!" Hannah said excitedly.

"How did that happen?" Francine exclaimed. "She hasn't spoken in years!"

"I don't know really. We were in her bedroom. I was playing my guitar, and she just started singing with me."

"That's wonderful news! I bet your whole family is ecstatic."

"That's for sure."

"I'm so flabbergasted and happy for little Ella."

"We all are," Hannah said.

"Okay, girly, now hit me with the bad news."

"It's Mom," Hannah said barely holding back her tears. "She has cancer, and it has spread throughout her body."

"Cancer? Well, there are treatments nowadays."

A heavy breath, laden with sorrow, escaped Hannah. "The doctors say that it has spread too far."

"Oh, poor Auntie Grace."

"I don't think that I'll be coming back to Montana. I want to be with Mom."

"I understand completely," Francine said. "But what about Travis?" Hannah sighed.

"I don't know."

"What do you mean you don't know? You're engaged to him."

Hannah said, her voice tinged with a mix of wonder and confusion, "You know, it's like I've been on this emotional roller coaster lately."

"What's going on?"

Hannah's shoulders fell as she breathed out slowly. "Remember how devastated I was after breaking up with Derek? I thought I'd never get over him."

"Yeah, you two were together forever, like since you were kids. It was tough watching you go through the breakup."

Hannah laid back on her pillow, lost in thought. "But then, out of nowhere, I met Travis. He was amazing, and things just seemed to click. It's been a whirlwind, honestly."

Interest piqued, Francine asked, "So you're happy with him?"

"I thought I was," Hannah admitted. "But lately, I find myself thinking more about Derek. It's like I can't fully let go. Is it crazy to still have feelings for him?"

Francine considered this. "It's not crazy, Hannah. He was a big part of your life. But do you miss him, or is it the idea of what you both had?"

Hannah mumbled, "I don't know. Travis is so different from Derek. Derek is caring and thinks about my feelings. I feel sometimes that Travis cares more about his parents and their horse ranch than me."

"In marriage, you have to think long term. After all, you will be spending a lifetime together."

Hannah bit her lip, contemplating. "That's just it. I'm not sure. I'm afraid of making the wrong choice."

"Listen, cousin, it isn't about making the perfect choice. It's about understanding what your heart truly wants. Give it time. You'll figure it out."

Hannah smiled; she felt like a weight had been lifted. "Thanks. I guess I just needed to hear that it's okay to be unsure."

"Always here for you, cousin. Just remember, it's your heart, your choice. No one else." Hannah said her goodbyes and then dialed Travis.

Hannah's voice trembled with a mixture of sorrow and resolve as she spoke to Travis over the phone, her words echoing in the empty room. "Travis, I…I can't come back to Montana for a while," she said softly, the weight of her decision heavy in her heart.

There was a pause, and then Travis's voice came through, laced with confusion and a hint of frustration. "Why not, Hannah? What's the ruckus?"

She took a deep breath, feeling the tears prick at the corners of her eyes. "It's my mom. She's…she's dying of cancer. I need to be with her, here in Tennessee. I need to be by her side during this time."

Travis's response was immediate, but it lacked the warmth and understanding she so desperately needed. "But, Hannah, how long you plannin' to be away? You do reckon you're gonna miss the winter festival: rodeo and roundup, ain't ya? It's the second grandest shindig of the year here in Montana."

The words stung Hannah like a slap in the face. She couldn't believe what she was hearing. Was he really talking about a rodeo at a time like this? Her voice rose, tinged with hurt and disbelief. "Travis, are you serious right now? I'm talking about my mother's life, her dying days, and all you can think about is a rodeo?"

There was a heavy silence on the other end of the line, and Hannah felt a cold realization settle over her. The man she was supposed to marry, the man she thought she knew, was showing her a side of himself she had suspected but didn't believe.

"Travis," she said, her voice breaking, "I thought you would understand. I thought you would be here for me, emotionally, not… not talking about some event."

Travis's voice softened, but it was too late. "I…I'm at a loss here. Why you gotta be away that long? What about everything tween us?"

Hannah closed her eyes, a single tear rolling down her cheek. "It's not about us right now. It's about my mom. And if you can't understand that, then…then maybe I've been wrong about us all along."

As she ended the call, the room seemed to close in around her, and she was left alone with her thoughts, the reality of her situation sinking in. Her mother's illness was changing everything, and maybe, just maybe, it was revealing truths she hadn't been willing to see before.

Chapter 8

In the warm, homey kitchen, the clatter of dishes punctuated the air as John gathered the breakfast dishes into the sink. Abby, her hands resting gently on her growing belly, offered to take over. "I'll wash those, Dad. You should relax with Mom in the living room."

John, placing the last dish into the sink and discarding the crumpled wrapping paper into the trash, decided to sit at the kitchen table instead. He looked toward Abby. The room, filled with the quiet hum of family life, set the stage for a heart-to-heart. "We haven't had much time to talk lately. How are you holding up?"

Abby, her face glowing with the radiance of impending motherhood, shared a slice of her life. "I'm doing well. Our doctor's happy with how the baby's progressing. And James, he's just thriving at work, possibly on the verge of becoming a senior partner at the law firm."

John's expression softened, a mix of concern and fatherly love. "I know your mom's illness has been tough on all of you. So tell me, really, how are you?"

Abby's voice wavered, a hint of vulnerability breaking through. "Of course, Mom's condition is heartbreaking. I pray for a miracle, like we had with Ella."

"That was indeed our Christmas miracle," John agreed, his voice tinged with nostalgia.

Abby's eyes brimmed with hidden sorrow. "I can't bear the thought of Mom not being here to meet her grandchild."

John, ever the optimist, reminded her, "You're only five months away from your due date, right?"

"Yes, but the doctors… They only gave Mom three," Abby whispered, the weight of her words heavy in the air.

John chuckled lightly, a twinkle in his eye. "Your mother's always been a fighter, stubborn to the core."

Abby, overcome by emotion, turned toward the sink, her back to her father. "I need to wash these dishes now."

John, reading the unspoken message, stood up, his heart full of paternal love. "I love you, honey."

Abby, her voice steady but soft, replied without turning around, "I love you too, Dad."

*****

Ella's movements were soft, almost reluctant, as she slid from the warmth of her mother's embrace. Her voice was a mere whisper, tinged with a quiet resolve. "I'm going to my room."

Her mother's response, gentle and undemanding, floated through the air. "Sure, sweetie," she said, her words laced with unspoken understanding. Grace watched Ella gather her things, her heart still carrying a warm feeling of the Christmas miracle of her little girl's voice returning. It gave Grace hope that miracles do happen.

Clutching the electronic tablet she had received for Christmas, a gift that now seemed trivial in the wake of her turmoil, Ella treaded silently down the hallway. Each step was measured, carrying the weight of her young heart.

As she entered her sanctuary, her eyes fell upon the painting—a stark reminder of her tumultuous emotions. In a moment of sorrow and anger, she had transformed the canvas into a chaotic reflection of her inner turmoil. With a heavy sigh, she carefully removed the marred painting from the easel, replacing it with a blank canvas, a symbol of a fresh start.

Settling on the edge of her bed, the comfort of familiar surroundings enveloped her. The paints and brushes, her loyal companions in expression, lay ready. She dipped her brush into the paint, the colors mingling and dancing at her command.

Slowly, with each deliberate stroke, a new image began to take shape. It was more than just painting on canvas; it was a testament to her resilience. A new picture of her family emerged, one filled with love, hope, and the promise of healing. In this silent communion with her art, Ella found her solace, her way back to peace.

*****

The soft glow of the Christmas tree reflected a festive mosaic of color on the window. The flickering light from the fireplace filled the room with its warmth. John and Grace lounged comfortably in their living room. Derek stood up from the couch, an electronic tablet cradled in his hands: a gift from the Gerards.

"I guess it's time for me to head out," Derek announced, his voice tinged with reluctance. He offered a warm, appreciative smile. "Thank you so much for the tablet. It's really amazing."

"You're always welcome here, Derek," Grace replied, her tone gentle and motherly.

John, nodding toward the tree, added, "Don't forget the gift for your folks. We wrapped it in that red and gold paper."

"Oh, right!" Derek said, his eyes lighting up as he picked up the festively decorated box. "Thanks again. They'll love it." He chuckled. "Whatever it is."

As Derek moved toward the door, his gaze drifted down the hallway, lingering, as if searching for something, or someone. The unspoken name hung in the air. With a subtle shake of his head and a faint, rueful smile, he turned back and stepped out the door.

The door clicked shut, leaving John and Grace alone with their thoughts. John broke the silence, his voice filled with a mix of affection and concern. "He sure is a good kid, isn't he?"

Grace leaned back, her eyes reflective. "Yes, he is. But did you notice? The way he looked down the hall. I think there's still something unresolved between him and Hannah."

John sighed, running a hand through his hair. "I've noticed it too. They've been like two peas in a pod since they were kids. It's hard seeing them like this now."

"Me too," Grace agreed softly. "I just hope they find a way to mend things. They've always been so good for each other."

John nodded, his gaze returning to the twinkling lights of the tree. "I hope so too. They both mean a lot to us."

Grace said, "True."

A light snow began to fall outside, the warmth of the fire in the fireplace gave the living room a comfortable feeling. John and Grace sat silently watching the flickering fire.

John finally broke the silence. "I think the girls are taking the bad news as well as can be expected," he murmured, his voice tinged with guilt.

Grace, her face etched with a quiet sadness, turned to him. "I can still see the sorrow and hurt in their eyes," she said gently. "I wanted to protect them from this pain, at least until Christmas was over."

John moved closer, his eyes reflecting a turmoil of emotions. "I know, but secrets have a way of festering. It's better they know, even if it hurts."

"But the timing, John, right before Christmas…" Grace's voice trailed off, her eyes brimming with tears.

John reached out, cradling her face in his hands. "I thought it was the right thing to do. To prepare them, to let them cherish the time left. Maybe I was wrong."

Grace leaned into his touch, a faint smile touching her lips. "You did what you thought was best. That's all we can ever do."

He pulled her close, enveloping her in a comforting embrace. "They're strong, like their mother. They'll cope, in their own ways."

"And we'll be there for them, like always," Grace whispered, resting her head on his shoulder.

John nodded, a determined glint in his eyes. "We'll make this Christmas the best one yet. Full of love, and joy, and memories to last a lifetime."

Grace pulled back slightly, looking up at him. "Let's promise to make every moment count, John. Not just for Christmas but for all the days we have left."

John kissed her forehead tenderly. "Every moment. Every single one."

In the silence that followed, filled with mutual understanding and love, the twinkling lights of the Christmas tree and the flickering light from the fireplace cast a soft glow around them, wrapping the couple in a cocoon of warmth and hope. For a while, they simply sat there, holding each other and letting the strength of their bond fortify them against the challenges ahead.

*****

Hannah lay sprawled on her bed, her mind a tumultuous sea of thoughts. She rose, feeling the weight of her recent conversation with Travis like a physical burden. Drifting into the living room, she sought Derek, her sanctuary in times of storm. But he wasn't there, its void echoing her inner desolation. She stood there, a figure of dejection, lost in her swirling thoughts.

In her loneliness, Derek's image loomed large. He was her rock, her haven of empathy and understanding. In contrast to Travis, Derek had the gift of making her feel valued and heard, a balm to her troubled spirit.

"Has Derek left?" Hannah queried, finding her parents, John and Grace, intertwined in solidarity.

"Just a moment ago," John replied, his voice a soft echo in the quiet room.

Grace, perceptive as always, probed gently, "What's happening with you two?"

"Nothing," Hannah responded, a whisper of denial, as she retreated to her room.

Back in her sanctuary, Hannah paced, her mind a whirlwind of memories and realizations. Derek, for all his flaws, was part of her, an integral thread in the tapestry of her life. As she pondered, the anger and hurt she harbored toward him started to dissipate, replaced by a yearning for the connection they once shared. Her heart, long guarded, began to thaw.

Hannah, feeling a whirlwind of emotions, dialed Derek's number. The phone rang, and Derek picked up.

Hannah said, "Derek? I…ah…just wanted to talk with you."

"Hey, Hannah. You sound upset. What's going on?"

Hannah's voice quivered slightly. "I…I've been thinking a lot. About us, about Travis. I feel like I've been lost, trying to hold onto something that isn't right for me."

"You mean with Travis?"

"Yes. With Travis, silly. With Travis, I always felt like I had to put on a show and be someone I'm not. But with you, it's always been different. You've always seen the real me."

Derek confessed, "I've always wanted you to be just that, yourself. That's the person I care about."

Hannah gave a soft sigh. "I know, and that means everything to me. I've made my decision. I'm going to return Travis's ring tomorrow. It's over between us."

Derek asked with concern, "Are you sure about this? I mean, I want you to be happy, Hannah, but only if you're sure."

"I'm sure. Being with Travis felt like I was constantly reaching for something that wasn't there. But you…you've always been my constant, my true north."

Derek said softly, "I've always been here for you, and I always will be. No matter what happens, that won't change."

"I know, and that's why I need to do this. To be fair to myself, to Travis, and maybe to us?"

Derek said, with a hopeful note in his voice, "Us?"

"Yes, Derek. I've realized that maybe the love I've been searching for has been right in front of me all along. You've been more than just a friend to me. You're a part of who I am."

"Hearing that…it means more than you know. I've always felt there's something special between us. I'm here for you, in whatever way you need."

"Thank you. Talking to you tonight, it's made me see things more clearly. I want to explore what this could mean for us, without any pretenses or masks."

"I'd like that, Hannah. Let's take it one step at a time. Whatever happens, we'll face it together."

Hannah ended the call, feeling a newfound sense of clarity and hope. The future might be uncertain, but one thing was clear: her journey was taking a new, promising turn.

Looking at her hand, Hannah slowly removed the ring Travis had given her, a symbol of a promise she could no longer keep. Resolved, she decided it was over between them. The ring would be returned tomorrow, a final closure to that chapter of her life.

Chapter 9

The knock on the front door echoed through the quaint, sunlit house. From the bustling kitchen, Abby's voice, infused with the warmth of home, called out, "I got it!" She dried her hands with the dish towel, and swinging the door open, she found herself staring, eyes wide and sparkling with unshed tears, at her husband James. The surprise etched on her face transformed into a radiant smile. "James! I thought you had to work," she exclaimed, her voice a blend of joy and incredulity.

James, his face lighting up at the sight of her, stepped forward, his voice soft yet filled with determination. "I took the red eye. Nothing could keep me away in your time of need."

Abby looped her arms around James, pulling him close. Her words were soft, almost lost in the fabric of his shirt. "You're always right where I need you," she murmured, her growing belly creating a gentle space between them. "But what about your big break? The senior partnership?"

James's fingers traced light patterns on her back. "Honey, some things are more important. Right here, with you and our little one," he said, his voice a soothing hum. "This," he gestured gently to her stomach, "is our future. Partnerships come and go, but family, that's forever."

Tears glistened in Abby's eyes as she looked up at him. "I'm scared. What if—"

He cut her off with a gentle finger to her lips. "No what ifs. We're in this together. Every step of the way. My promotion can wait. Right now, this moment with you, is all that matters."

Abby's eyes shone with a mix of fear and love. "You're incredible, you know that?"

James chuckled softly, his eyes crinkling with affection. "I'm just a guy in love with his wife and unborn child. Nothing more, nothing less."

Hand in hand, Abby led James into the living room, where her parents, John and Grace, were sitting in a silent embrace. The air was heavy with unspoken emotions, a mixture of sadness and love.

John rose to his feet, a surprised smile creasing his weathered face. "Well, this is a pleasant surprise," John said. "Welcome home, son." John's handshake was firm, a testament to a lifetime of hard work and resilience.

Grace, her smile gentle yet tinged with the weariness of her battle, remained seated. Her eyes, however, sparkled with a fierce strength. James bent down to hug her, his voice tinged with respect and sorrow.

"I'm so sorry, Grace. I wish I could do more."

Grace's laugh, though strained, was filled with warmth. "Thank you. But remember, I'm still here, fighting."

Abby, her eyes flicking between James and her parents, asked, "How long can you stay?"

James, his expression torn between duty and love, replied, "A couple of days. Then I must return. But every moment here counts."

John's voice, filled with gratitude, broke the brief silence. "We're all just glad you could be here. It means more than you know."

The room, filled with the complex tapestry of family—love, sacrifice, and the strength found in togetherness—seemed to embrace them all, a reminder that in the face of life's hardest trials, they were not alone.

*****

Weeks later, Grace, looking frail but spirited, was seated on the couch. John, her husband, was beside her, holding her hand. Hannah and Ella, their daughters, were nearby, with Hannah's boyfriend, Derek, in their renewed relationship.

John squeezed Grace's hand gently. "Every day with you, Grace, is a gift. We're all here for you, every step of the way."

Grace smiled weakly. "I know. I feel so blessed to have all of you. You're my strength."

Hannah said, "Mom, you've always been our rock. It's our turn to be yours. We'll get through this together."

Ella said, "Yeah, Mom. Hannah's right. We're here, always."

Derek, being supportive, said, "Mrs. G, you've been like a second mother to me. I'm here for you and the family, whatever you need."

*****

Months later, James fiddled nervously with his pocket, feeling for the ring, as he stood at the altar beside Derek. A quick glance across Derek, and there was Abby, looking stunning in her bridesmaid's gown, a spitting image of the day they first met. Her baby bulge looked like it was going to pop any day now. His lips curled into a smile.

The melodious strains of Wagner's "Bridal Chorus" filled the air, prompting everyone to rise. Derek's eyes widened, taking in Hannah, breathtaking in her white gown, gliding down the aisle, her arm linked with her father, John. *She's more radiant than ever,* he thought, his heart skipping a beat.

At the altar's steps, John tenderly lifted Hannah's veil, planting a soft kiss on her cheek. With a beaming smile, Hannah ascended the steps toward Derek, sharing a warm glance with her sister, Abby, before clasping Derek's hand. John retreated, joining Grace, his wife, who sat proudly in her wheelchair, a stylish hat gracefully hiding the traces of her battle with cancer. Her camera laid on her lap.

Hannah, her eyes shimmering behind the delicate veil, gazed at Derek. *He's my dashing James Bond,* she mused, *ready to sweep me off to some exotic locale. Who knew we'd reunite like this? Seems the Lord always had this plan for us.*

Their vows exchanged, they sealed their union with a deep, meaningful kiss, encapsulating their journey from friends to soulmates. The guests erupted in applause as the newlyweds made their way down the aisle, hand in hand, toward their future together. Grace snapped a picture. Hannah, seeing the flash, smiled, another memory captured by her mother.

The reception was a whirlwind of joy—laughter, dancing, heartfelt wishes. Hannah twirled on the dance floor with Derek, her heart soaring. Leaning close, she whispered, "This is just the beginning, love."

Halfway through the reception, John gestured for Derek to follow him outside. "What's on your mind, Mr. G?" Derek asked curiously.

John's hand rested gently on Derek's shoulder. "Call me Dad now. You're family."

Derek stumbled, "Yes, Mr. G, I mean…Dad."

John spoke earnestly, "I've always longed for a son to join me in the family lumber business, especially after my father passed. Grace and I were blessed with daughters and a surprise little Ella later. But now, I want you to consider joining the family business."

Derek hesitated. "But the Taylor Christmas Tree Farm. I think my father wanted me to take that over for him someday."

John chuckled. "Why not both? The tree farm is mainly seasonal, and after all, they are kindred trades."

Derek nodded, a new warmth in his voice, "That makes perfect sense, Dad."

*****

The Gerard family's living room was a picture of heartache and weariness. John, the patriarch, sat slumped in his favorite armchair, his eyes lost in the void of his thoughts. Across from him, Hannah clutched a crumpled tissue, her face etched with the fatigue of endless nights. Beside her, little Ella hugged her knees to her chest, her innocence shadowed by the grim reality encircling their family.

"It's getting too much," John's voice was hoarse, weighed down by a decision he never thought he'd have to make. "Your mother's condition… She needs more care than we can give."

Hannah nodded, her voice thick with emotion. "I found her on the floor last night, Dad. She fell trying to get to the bathroom. And…and when she looks at me, sometimes there's just confusion. She doesn't always recognize me."

John's face crumpled. "She's in pain too. The medications aren't working like they used to. And the doctors…they say it's only going to get worse."

Ella's voice, small and trembling, cut through the heavy air. "She can't eat her food anymore. I tried to make her favorite soup, but she just couldn't."

Hannah found herself torn between the demands of her personal life and the profound responsibility of caring for her ailing mother. Hannah confided in her father, her voice laden with the weight of her dilemma. "Between my husband, Derek, and my job at the music store, I feel like I'm failing both by spending so much time here. Derek understands, but I can see the strain it's putting on our relationship. And work… I'm barely holding on. Besides, Mom's condition is deteriorating. It's reaching a point beyond what non-medical people like us can manage effectively. I can't keep doing this. It's tearing me apart."

John reached out, encompassing his daughter's hands in his. "Hospice recommended a hospital stay. They can manage her pain, keep her comfortable. It's not what we wanted, but…"

"But it's what's best for Mom," Hannah finished, a tear rolling down her cheek. "She always said she didn't want us to see her suffer. We've been trying, but we're not enough, not for this."

Ella sniffed. "Will she be alone there?"

"We'll be with her, every step of the way," John assured, his voice firm. "We'll visit, talk to her, be there for her. We can't take away her pain, but we can make sure she's not alone through it."

Hannah wiped her eyes, standing up with a newfound resolve. "I'll call the hospital. We'll bring her things and make her room feel like home. Photos, her favorite blanket. She needs to know we're still with her, even there."

The room, once filled with despair, slowly shifted to a space of collective strength. A family bound by love facing the toughest decision, but united in their commitment to ensure Grace's final days were enveloped in the comfort and dignity she deserved.

*****

The sun streamed gently through the curtains of Grace's bedroom, casting a warm, comforting glow over the room. Grace lay propped up in bed, a frail shadow of her former self, yet her eyes still held the same spark of determination that had always defined her.

John stood by the bed, his heart heavy with the task at hand. Hannah and Ella flanked him, their faces a mix of bravery and apprehension. The room was filled with tense anticipation, as if the walls themselves were bracing for the conversation ahead.

"Grace," John began, his voice trembling slightly. "We need to talk about something important."

Grace looked at her family, a sense of unease flickering across her face. "What is it, John?" she asked, her voice weaker than she intended.

John took a deep breath, choosing his words with care. "Your health, it's getting more difficult for us to manage here at home. You need constant care, more than what we can provide."

Grace's expression turned to one of mild defiance. "I don't want to go anywhere. This is my home! My family is here. I want to stay!"

Hannah stepped forward, her eyes glistening with tears not fallen. "Mom, we know this is hard. But last night, when you fell, we were so scared. We can't bear the thought of something happening to you and us not being able to help."

Ella spoke softly, "Mom, I don't like seeing you in pain. The doctors at the hospital can make you feel better."

John reached out, taking Grace's hand in his. "We're not leaving you. We'll visit you every day. You won't be alone, not for a moment. We just want what's best for you."

Grace looked into the earnest faces of her family, her resolve wavering. "But a hospital... It's so cold, so impersonal. I don't want my last days to be in a place like that."

"We'll make it feel like home, Mom," Hannah promised. "We'll bring your favorite blanket, the family photos. We'll be there with you, just like we are here."

Grace's eyes filled with tears as the reality of her situation sank in. "I'm scared," she whispered, a vulnerability in her voice that was rare.

John squeezed her hand tighter. "We're scared too. But we're in this together, always. You won't have to face anything alone."

The room was quiet for a moment, the only sound being the soft ticking of the clock on the wall. Finally, Grace nodded slowly, a sign of her trust and love for her family.

"Okay," she said softly, "I'll go. For you, for all of you. But promise me, stay with me. Don't let me be alone."

"We promise," John said, a tear rolling down his cheek. "We'll be with you, every step of the way."

As the family gathered around Grace, holding onto each other, a new chapter in their journey began. It was one filled with uncertainty and sorrow but also with the unbreakable bond of a family united in love and commitment.

*****

A week later, in Nashville General Hospital, John—her steady companion—sat next to Grace's bed. "Is she…?" John's voice was barely a whisper, his eyes never leaving Grace's peaceful face.

"Soon," the hospice nurse replied softly, her eyes sympathetic. "Very soon. She's been a fighter."

The nurse left the room. The hospital room was silent, except for the soft hum of machines and the faint bleeps that were now sporadic. Grace—lying there with oxygen tubes and monitoring wires, her eyes closed—seemed almost serene. The cancer that had ravaged her body had not been able to touch her spirit.

James with Abby, holding her week-old baby, Olivia, stepped into the hospital room.

John greeted them. "I'm so glad you were able to make it."

"How's Mom?" Abby asked.

John shook his head, tears wetting his eyes.

Abby, with the baby in her arms, stepped forward tentatively. Tears glistened in her eyes. "Mom?" Her voice cracked, a mixture of hope and despair.

Grace's eyes fluttered open, a weak but genuine smile spreading across her lips as she saw her granddaughter. "Olivia…" she murmured, her voice a tender caress. "The Kodak…"

John squeezed Grace's hand, tears streaming down his face. "You did it, Grace. You held on to see her."

The monitors bleeped a warning, and a nurse rushed in, her steps quick but soundless. She checked the screens, her face turning solemn. "I need the doctor, stat," she said into her walkie-talkie, her voice calm but urgent.

The room seemed to hold its breath as the doctor entered, his expression grave. He checked the screens then gently felt Grace's pulse. With a heavy heart, he slowly raised the sheet over her head.

John's body shook with silent sobs, his head bowed in grief. Abby clutched her baby closer, tears falling freely. James placed his hand around Abby's shoulders.

"She knew," Abby whispered through her tears. "She knew Olivia was here."

John looked up, his eyes meeting Abby's. "She held on for this moment," he said, his voice thick with emotion. "She was waiting to see her grandbaby."

As they gathered around and prayed, the room was filled with a profound sense of loss but also a deep love that transcended even death. Grace had left them, but in her final moments, she had witnessed the continuation of her family, a final testament to her enduring strength and love.

Chapter 10

In the hushed stillness of the funeral, the air was laden with a heart-rending blend of grief and enduring affection. A modest assembly of mourners united in their sorrow formed a half-circle around the casket, an unspoken testament to the life and legacy of Grace. Her family, a portrait of stoic heartache, stood prominently at the forefront, their faces a canvas of memories and unvoiced regrets. Behind them, a sea of friends and church parishioners, each silently grappling with their own sense of loss, offered a quiet homage.

Faith, Grace's older sister, her eyes brimming with tears, stood silently beside her husband Jordan, their hands tightly clasped as if drawing strength from one another. Their daughter Francine, acutely aware of the gravity of the moment, clung to her parents, her face a mirror of their grief. Her Aunt Grace had always been loving toward her.

Faith glanced over at her nieces, the pain in her heart mirrored in their eyes. "I can't believe she's gone," she whispered to Jordan, her voice barely audible. Jordan, a pillar of support, wrapped his arm around her shoulders, offering a silent comfort that words could not convey.

Abby, cradling Olivia in her arms, tried to paint a picture of the grandmother Olivia would never know. "Your Grandma Grace, she had this way of making every story come alive," she said, her voice gentle yet quivering with emotion. Olivia lay cradled in the warmth of her mother's embrace. Words, soft and gentle, cascaded over her; though the language was yet a mystery to her infant mind, the love in her mother's voice was as clear and comforting as the embrace that held her close.

James, Abby's husband, offered a comforting presence, his hand resting gently on Abby's back. "She lives on through us, through these stories we'll share with Olivia," he said softly, his words a soothing balm to their aching hearts.

Nearby, Hannah leaned into Derek, finding solace in his embrace. "Mom always believed in celebrating life, even in its end," she whispered, a tear escaping her eye.

Derek, his own eyes glistening, nodded in agreement. "She lived with such joy, such grace. We honor her by living the same way," he replied, his voice filled with a mix of sorrow and respect.

Ella held a photo of their mother close to her heart. "Do you think Mom's watching us from the stars?" she asked, her voice tinged with a child's hopeful curiosity.

Abby knelt beside her, pulling her into a gentle hug. "Mom is in heaven now with Grandma. They're with Jesus, waiting for us to join her someday." Abby reassured her, finding a semblance of peace in her belief.

Overwhelmed by a torrent of sorrow, John approached the casket, a poignant portrait of heartache etched upon his features. Gently, he laid a solitary rose atop the solemn casket, its delicate petals a stark contrast to the finality it represented. Words failed him, his voice stifled by the weight of his loss.

Leaning closer, he whispered a tender final farewell to his cherished wife and friend of thirty years, a whisper carrying the depth of their shared love and the pain of their untimely parting.

Pastor Elijah Wilson's solemn voice broke through their reflections. "Today, we say farewell to Grace, a remarkable woman whose kindness and love touched us all," he said, his words echoing the deep loss they all felt. "Second Corinthians, chapter five verse eight tells us that to be absent from the body is to be present with the Lord. A place where I am sure sister Grace is now smiling."

As the casket was lowered, the family's collective sob filled the air, a heart-wrenching sound of farewell. The three sisters, united in their sorrow, let their tears flow, each drop a testament to their love and the profound impact their mother had on their lives. In this moment of final goodbye, they clung to each other, finding comfort in the shared love and memories of a woman who had been their guiding light.

Later that day, the room was draped in a soft, comforting glow, the kind that only comes from a gathering of hearts united in loss and love. Grace Gerard's wake, held in the spacious living room of her home, was a blend of somber reflection and gentle laughter, a testament to a life lived with kindness and warmth.

Faith, a mirror image of Grace in her younger years, stood near the fireplace, her eyes scanning the room filled with church members, friends, and family. Her gaze rested on Grace's husband, John, who sat quietly in an armchair, his face a portrait of stoic sadness. Beside him, Grace's daughters, each a different shade of their mother, huddled together, finding solace in shared sorrow.

Abby held her two-week-old baby, Olivia, close to her chest. "Little Olivia will hear so many stories about her grandmother."

James, her husband, nodded, "Your mom would have adored her. She was so excited to be a grandmother."

Abby said, "Mom would have loved this, all of us together. She always said family is where love never ends."

James squeezed her hand. "She's here, Abby, in every story we share, in every laugh we remember." Across the room, Hannah and her husband Derek stood by the window, reminiscing. "Mom taught me so much," Hannah said softly. "How to love." Their eyes met. "How to forgive."

Derek wrapped an arm around her. "She lives on through you, Hannah. Through all of us."

Ella, the youngest at eleven, sat on the floor, her small frame curled up with a photo album of her mother. John watched her, a bittersweet smile on his lips. "Grace loved those photos," he remarked to the pastor who had joined him.

Pastor Wilson nodded. "She captured moments, not just pictures. Her legacy is in these memories."

As the evening wore on, the room filled with stories of Grace—her laughter, her wisdom, her unwavering faith. Friends from church shared tales of her kindness, her unwavering support, and her ability to make everyone feel loved.

"Grace had a way of seeing the best in people," one of the church members said. "She lifted us up, always believing in us."

As the wake drew to a close, John gathered everyone for a final prayer. Holding hands, they formed a circle, a symbol of the unbroken bond they shared with Grace and with each other. John nodded to the pastor. "Pastor."

"Though we grieve," Pastor Wilson began, his voice steady, "and although she's not here, we know that she is now in glory with our Lord and Savior Jesus Christ. Therefore, celebrate her life beautifully lived. Grace's love surrounds us still, guiding us, holding us. In her memory, we find strength. Amen."

The room echoed with soft amens, and as they released hands, there was a sense of peace, a feeling that Grace Gerard, in her quiet, loving way, had left an indelible mark on each of them—a whisper of grace that would linger in their hearts forever.

Chapter 11

As the sun dipped low in the sky, casting long shadows over Gerard Lumber Yard, John Gerard locked his office, his steps echoing in the quiet of the closing hour. He was making his way to his truck when Derek called out.

"Headed to fetch Ella from school?" Derek inquired with a friendly grin.

"Exactly," John replied, a hint of warmth in his voice. "Hannah's caught up at the music store downtown and can't make it in time."

"Yeah, she's teaching guitar lessons, and she didn't know if she was getting a new student or not."

"Evidently, she did. I'm glad she's doing well," John said, turning to his truck.

As John was opening the truck door, Derek raised his hand, signaling a pause. "Hold up, before you leave, I've got a hilarious story from today."

Intrigued, John paused, his face a canvas of curiosity. He had seen Derek adapt swiftly to the rhythms of the yard, a quick learner with a knack for the trade. "What's up?"

Derek's smile broadened, his eyes twinkling with mirth. "So Old Man Jonesy strolls in, wanting some two by fours," he began, barely containing his laughter. "I asked him, 'How long do you need them?' And, oh, you'll love this. He says, 'Well, I reckon a long time. I'm fixing up my barn.' You know, as in 'how long a length'?"

A chuckle escaped John's lips. "That's ole Jonesy, all right." His expression turned more serious. "But remember, he's a loyal customer. Treat him well."

Derek's smile faltered slightly, replaced by a nod of understanding. "Oh, I did. Once we got past the mix-up, he told me the exact lengths he needed."

John nodded approvingly. "I'm sure you handled it well. You're a good kid, son." With that, he opened the door to his pickup, ready to leave.

Derek waved him off, returning to his tasks. "Give my regards to Ella!"

"I will," John promised, settling into his truck and driving away, the day's work behind him and family time ahead.

*****

Gerard Lumber Yard's sign, adorning the side of a pickup truck, signifies more than just a business—it was his legacy. John Gerard, faced with a pivotal decision years ago, chose family over personal ambition. His father, the heart of the family lumber mill, was ill and needed him. John's choice was unwavering: family over everything was his motto.

The allure of athletic stardom, with its roaring crowds and glittering stadium lights, was strong. However, John was drawn more powerfully to the lumber mill, driven by a deep sense of responsibility and familial love. He exchanged the adrenaline of sports for the earthy aroma of sawdust, a decision that reflected his profound commitment to his family's heritage.

John's departure from Tennessee State University's football program marked the loss of a gifted athlete, but for him, the steady hum of saws slicing through timber was a melody far more meaningful than any stadium cheer. The lumber mill, a testament to hard work and family bonds, had been nurtured through four generations.

John's sacrifice bore fruit as he immersed himself in the mill's operations, guided by his father and seasoned workers. This path led him to discover a profound sense of fulfillment, with the mill's rhythms becoming his anthem and the sweet smell of sawdust a reminder of his father's teachings.

John's journey was a departure from his initial dreams, yet it led him to a different form of greatness: one defined by love, sacrifice, and a steadfast connection to his roots.

Side by side with his father until the latter's passing, John's resolve only strengthened. He had taken over the lumber business, transforming it through relentless effort and dedication into a thriving enterprise, a symbol of his resilience.

John's pickup truck pulled up into the line in front of the school. John still wore the ring of his dearly departed wife. Grace had passed away six months ago in June of this year. The school bell rang, and children came pouring out the doors of Rosa Parks Elementary school (formally Robert E. Lee Elementary School). The pickup truck moved slowly ahead as parents picked up their children. John saw Ella waving to him as she said goodbye to her friends. *Ella talking,* John thought, *is still a miracle to me.*

Ella, buzzing with the energy of an eleven-year-old, hopped into the truck, her eyes shining with the excitement of the upcoming break. "No more school for two weeks!" she exclaimed, her voice a mix of relief and anticipation.

John smiled at her enthusiasm. "I remember feeling the same way about Christmas vacation," he said, the term feeling natural and nostalgic.

"It's called winter break, Dad," Ella corrected gently, a playful tone in her voice.

John chuckled. "Well, to me, it'll always be Christmas vacation. But you're right, it's a whole two-week break without school for you."

As they drove past groups of children, Ella waved to her friends. "Sometimes I wish school didn't let out. I'm going to miss them," she said, a hint of sadness in her voice. "Now that my voice has returned, it is easier making new friends."

"You'll see them soon enough," John reassured her. "And don't forget, your sister and the baby will be home for the holidays. That's something to look forward to."

Ella's face lit up at the mention of her niece. "I can't wait to see little Olivia! I'm going to be the best auntie ever," she declared with pride.

John's heart warmed to her excitement. "I have no doubt about that. And who knows, maybe we can all build a snowman together if we get enough snow."

Ella's eyes sparkled at the idea. "That would be awesome! Can we use some of your tools from the lumberyard to make it the coolest snowman ever?"

"Sure, we can do that. Maybe we'll make it the talk of the neighborhood," John said, the corners of his eyes crinkling with a smile.

As the truck neared their home, Ella's thoughts turned to her mother. "Do you think Mom would have liked Olivia?" she asked softly.

John's heart ached a bit at the mention of Grace, but he answered gently, "Your mom would have adored her. Just like she adored all of you."

Ella nodded, looking out the window. "I miss her, Dad."

"I do too, sweetheart, every day. But she's always with us, in our hearts and in the memories we share," John said, reaching over to give Ella's hand a reassuring squeeze.

Ella squeezed back, a small smile returning to her face. "I love you, Dad."

"I love you too, Ella. Always," John replied, his voice full of affection.

*****

Ella gazed wistfully at the snowflakes twirling gracefully outside the living room window, her heart heavy with the absence of her mother this Christmas. Suddenly, her face brightened as she spotted a car approaching. "Hannah's here!" she exclaimed, her voice echoing with excitement and a hint of relief.

Her father, John, joined her at the front door, his footsteps steady and comforting. "Hurry up, come on in," he called out to Derek and Hannah as they emerged from their car. Like Santa Claus, Derek hoisted a black plastic bag over his shoulder, laden with gifts.

Hannah's laughter rang through the cold air. "Yeah, we can't afford to warm up all of Tennessee!" she joked, her voice warm and teasing.

John's laughter mingled with hers. "That's right. I see that married life has given you a little wisdom," he teased back, his eyes crinkling with mirth.

"Well, when you have to pay your own utility bills, you learn all about your father's wisdom," Hannah retorted playfully as they stepped inside, brushing snow from their coats.

The moment Hannah was within reach, John enveloped her in a big fatherly hug. "How have you been feeling?" he asked, his tone softening with concern.

Hannah smiled, her hand resting on her slightly bulging stomach. "Little Elizabeth Grace Taylor is causing me a little nausea, but other than that, the baby and I are fine," she replied, her voice filled with a mix of discomfort and joy.

Ella wrapped her arms around Hannah, bending to speak to her stomach. "I can hardly wait to see you, little… What shall we call her?" she asked, her voice filled with wonder and anticipation.

"We were thinking that Gracie would be a good nickname for the baby," Hannah suggested, her eyes glowing with affection.

Ella nodded thoughtfully. Then, her gaze drifting to the family picture over the fireplace, she murmured, "I think mom would have liked that." Her voice was tinged with nostalgia and a faint sadness.

Derek, who had been admiring the picture Ella had painted, nodded in agreement. "Nice," he said, his voice filled with admiration for the family portrait.

John, ever the patriarch, announced, "I asked Ella to paint a new one to include James, Olivia, and of course, you, Derek. After all, we're all family." His voice was brimming with pride and inclusiveness.

Derek chuckled. "Maybe she ought to hold off on that until little Gracie is born." His voice carried a light-hearted, teasing tone.

"I have a feeling that there are going to be many revisions in the future," John said, his voice filled with a sense of inevitable change and growth.

As Derek began placing the Christmas presents under the tree, Ella's excitement couldn't be contained. "Abby is here!" she squealed, her voice bubbling with joy at the arrival of her sister and niece.

Abby, with little Olivia in her arms, and James, struggling with suitcases, were greeted warmly. "How was your flight?" John asked, his voice filled with genuine interest as he hugged his daughter and planted a kiss on Olivia's forehead.

"Perfect. Olivia was a good girl on the airplane," Abby replied, her voice filled with maternal pride, while Olivia beamed, oblivious yet happy.

Ella's excitement was palpable, her youthful squeal echoing through the room as she caught sight of her adorable niece. With an energy only an eleven-year-old could muster, she dashed over, her eyes sparkling with delight. Gently, she scooped up little Olivia into a tender embrace, cradling her with the utmost care. Olivia, at seven months, was a bundle of joy, her tiny hand clasping Ella's finger with innocent curiosity.

"Can I show Olivia the Christmas tree?" Ella's voice was tinged with eagerness, her gaze turning toward the festively adorned living room.

Abby, watching over them with a protective yet loving gaze, nodded, a soft smile playing on her lips.

"Yes, but be careful."

Under Abby's watchful eyes, Ella carefully carried Olivia into the living room. The Christmas tree stood tall and magnificent, its lights twinkling like stars in a clear night sky. Ella's excitement was infectious as she pointed out each decoration to Olivia, her words a gentle melody of wonder. The highlight was the shelf elf on the mantle, a symbol of their cherished family traditions.

"This is Petey," Ella said, smiling and pointing to the worn, color-faded red-and-white shelf elf. "Mysteriously, he appears all over the house every morning."

Olivia, merely seven months into the world, greeted the moment with a smile, her innocence and lack of understanding only amplifying the charm of her expression. Ella, her aunt—a youthful spirit at eleven—radiated a joy so infectious, so bright, that it seemed to light up the very air around her. In that shared space, their bond was palpable, a beautiful intertwining of youth and new life, where Olivia's smile, unknowing yet pure, reflected the unbridled enthusiasm that Ella brought into the room.

Abby watched, her heart swelling with pride and love. In this simple, beautiful moment, she saw the continuation of traditions that had always brought their family together. The connection between Ella and Olivia was more than just that of aunt and niece: it was a promise of future joys, shared experiences, and the enduring warmth of family love.

James went back to the car for another load of suitcases and presents. Derek walked out to help him. With arms overloaded with luggage and brightly wrapped boxes, they came back into the house. They dropped the suitcases in the hallway and put the Christmas presents under the tree.

James, rejoining the family, laughed at Derek. "You'll soon find out when you have a baby. It's like being a moving company whenever you go anyplace," he joked, his voice light but hinting at the chaos of traveling with a child.

"I'm looking forward to it," Derek responded, his voice indicating he was both amused and earnest about the joys and challenges of impending fatherhood.

John and James looked at each other and started to laugh. John said, "He'll learn."

The Gerard family, now altogether, sat around the living room, enjoying each other's company in the twinkling lights of the Christmas tree and the flickering light from the fireplace. Their laughter echoed through the home, a symphony of joy and kinship that painted the air with the essence of Christmas. It was a time of creating new memories, a season wrapped in the comfort of togetherness.

Life's eternal dance of beginnings and ends whispered softly amidst their celebrations, a gentle reminder of life's fragile beauty. Miracles, those elusive gifts from the Lord, sometimes graced their lives, though answers from the heavens weren't always clothed in affirmation. Sometimes they came as a no or a patient wait. In these moments, they learned to anchor their hearts in unwavering faith, trusting in a plan greater than their own.

John started to leave the room, saying, "We have to take a family picture."

Hannah said to her departing father, "No need to get that old camera. I have my cellphone."

"I got it covered," John said as he returned with the tripod. "Gather around the fireplace for a family picture."

John positioned his cellphone on the tripod and adjusted the timer. He hurried to join the warm, growing circle of his family, their faces alight with anticipation. As the camera captured the moment, a burst of laughter echoed through the air.

Hannah's laughter was bright and teasing as she glanced at her father's new cellphone, a stark contrast to the vintage Kodak camera of old. "Welcome to the twenty-first century, Dad," she quipped, her eyes sparkling with mirth.

John's smile, tinged with a touch of nostalgia, warmed the group. "I'm certain your mom would've approved," he murmured, his voice a blend of fondness and memory.

Hannah looked at the ceiling and laughed. "No lightning bolts, so I guess you're right, Dad."

END

About the Author

A Purple Heart veteran and father of five, Bob Leone lives in the San Francisco Bay Area. He is an accomplished author, film producer, cartoonist, and painter. His company, Inspireworks LLC, has produced films like *They Don't Cast Shadows* and their latest, *December to Remember*. You can see his work at his website: www.aimhigherbooks.com.